BITE ME!

SARAH MICHELLE GELLAR

AND

BUFFY THE VAMPIRE SLAYER

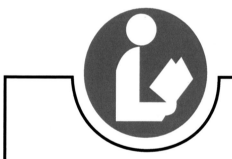

BITE ME!

Sarah Michelle Gellar
and
Buffy the Vampire Slayer

NIKKI STAFFORD

ECW PRESS
OCM 39354970

CANADIAN CATALOGUING IN PUBLICATION DATA

Stafford, Nikki, 1973–

Bite Me! Sarah Michelle Gellar and Buffy the Vampire Slayer

Includes bibliographical references.
ISBN 1-55022-361-5

1. Gellar, Sarah Michelle, 1977– . 2. Buffy the vampire slayer (Television
program). 3. Television actors and actresses – United States – Biography.
I. Title. II. Title: Buffy the vampire slayer.

PN2287.g44572 1998   791.45'028'092   C98-930947-9

Cover design by Guylaine Régimbald.
Design and imaging by ECW Type & Art, Oakville, Ontario.
Printed and bound by Printcrafters, Winnipeg, Manitoba.
Distributed in Canada by General Distribution Services,
30 Lesmill Road, Don Mills, Ontario M3B 2T6.
Distributed in the United States by LPC Group,
1436 West Randolph Street, Chicago, Illinois, U.S.A. 60607.
Distributed in the United Kingdom by Turnaround Publisher Services,
Unit 3 Olympia Trading Estate, Coburg Road, Wood Green, London N2Z 6TZ

Published by ECW PRESS,
2120 Queen Street East, Suite 200,
Toronto, Ontario M4E 1E2.
www.ecw.ca/press

PRINTED AND BOUND IN CANADA

TABLE OF CONTENTS

ACKNOWLEDGMENTS

I would like to take this opportunity to thank all of the people who have helped me out while I've been working on this book. Although only one name appears on the cover as the author, books like this are often the result of the work of many helpers.

First, I would like to thank the people from the *Buffy the Vampire Slayer* posting board, who gave me a tremendous amount of help on the *Buffy* posting board party chapter: Erika Rottler (a.k.a. Sasheer), Viet My Nyugen (a.k.a. Samiel), Karri Phillips (a.k.a. Phoenix), Keith Miller (a.k.a. KAM), Erika Gilbert (a.k.a. Batra), Tammie Purcell (a.k.a. greengirl), and Will York (a.k.a. fenric). A special thank-you to Erika Rottler, Karri, Samiel, and Keith for supplying the photos that were used to illustrate the chapter.

Thanks to Lisa Rose for providing some photos for the book, Sonja Marie Isaacs for giving me information about the Anthony Stewart Head fan club, and Leslie Remencus for letting me use information from her Web site for the episode guide. A warm thank-you to Scott Robinson (a.k.a. Lawless) for reading over the initial manuscript and fact-checking the biography section, and for providing so many useful articles on his Web site.

I would like to thank Robert Lecker at ECW Press for giving me this wonderful opportunity, as well as the generous people who work with the company: Holly Potter, Jennifer Trainor, Jack David, Guylaine Régimbald, Megan Ferrier, and Paul Davies. A big thanks to Stuart Ross, my invaluable editor, for doing such a terrific job with the manuscript.

Thanks also to everyone who has been so supportive of me in this and other endeavors: Jonathan and Johanne Hale, Robert Thompson, Jeremy Barker, Sheila Rusticus, Chris Lockett, Julie Ruffell, Marion McLarty, Mike D'Angelo, Christine Samuelian, John Hale, Sarah Thompson, Anjali Kapoor, Shanda Deziel, Andy Poon, Albert Wisco, Sandy, Piquette, Sebastian, and all of my family and friends. A special thank-you to Kim Koller, a true friend and my #1 fan. As always, my biggest thanks are reserved for Jennifer Hale, who always offers her most generous help in everything I do.

This book is dedicated to *Buffy* fans everywhere.

INTRODUCTION

SLAYERS AND WATCHERS:
A NEW VAMPIRE MYTHOLOGY

Buffy the Vampire Slayer first aired on March 10, 1997, and
immediately exceeded everyone's expectations. Based on
a largely unsuccessful film about a high school girl whose
calling is to rid the world of demons, it carried with it the
stigma that it would be a stupid television series for kids
that was uncreative and imitative. Many people, including
those who worked on the show, weren't sure it would last
beyond the first season. But it did, and it continued to gain
popularity among both fans and critics.

Vampires, in both fiction and folklore, have fascinated
readers and moviegoers for centuries. With the advent of
Bram Stoker's *Dracula* in 1897, the legend of the vampire
moved into the mainstream, and in the twentieth century
Dracula became a movie icon. *Nosferatu* (1922) was the
first of the major vampire movies, but it was Bela Lugosi,
in Tod Browning's 1931 *Dracula*, who forever changed the
idea of a monstrous demon into a more sexual metaphor.
Dracula became suave and sophisticated, and his attacks
on the necks of defenseless women were likened to a
seduction. It was this image of the vampire as seducer that
prevailed, reaching new peaks in the Anne Rice novels of

the 1980s and '90s, which featured a romantic yet vicious vampire named Lestat. In 1992, *Bram Stoker's Dracula*, starring Gary Oldman and Winona Ryder, revived the idea of the vampire as a monster, remaining truer to Stoker's vision than most of the adaptations before it. In that same year, Fran Rubel Kuzui's *Buffy the Vampire Slayer* was released, starring Kristy Swanson and Luke Perry, which added a new element to the vampire legend — the idea that someone exists to rid the world of vampires.

The fiction involving vampires contains significantly different conventions than the folklore. For example, in the vampire fiction, you become a vampire only if bitten by one. In the folklore, however, it was believed that someone could become a vampire if an animal leapt over their coffin; if they'd been murdered or had committed suicide; if they'd been born with a harelip, or on Saturday, or between Christmas and Epiphany; if they'd been buried alive; if they hadn't been buried properly; and in other ways. In fiction, the vampire tends to be a rich nobleman with a lot of money; in folklore, it's a poor peasant wandering the countryside. In movies, the vampire is tall, thin, and debonair, with a cape, a white face, and sharp teeth. In the folklore the vampire has rosy-colored skin and is bloated because of all the blood he has drunk; his teeth are rarely mentioned; his left eye — or both — are wide open and staring, even while he's asleep during the day. In fiction, when the body of the vampire is staked it disappears or mummifies; in folklore, the corpse must be disposed of. It was sometimes believed that the staking alone would not work, so the act was followed up with the cremation of the body. In both, vampires are more often male than female, and in the folklore the only female vampires are mothers who died in childbirth.

The folklore surrounding the vampire legend was actually based on real-life fears. Some aspects of the vampire

legend were invented during plagues — when people in a
particular area died in large numbers, the townspeople
would sometimes rationalize the deaths by blaming the
first person who died. They would say that at night he
roamed from house to house and sucked the life from
people, who would be found dead the next day. These
stories would prompt doctors to exhume the body of the
first victim and stake it, and some medical reports of
the time state that the hair and nails had been growing and
blood came out like a river when they staked the body.
There have since been many scholarly explanations for the
doctors' "findings." When the skin begins to decompose,
it shrinks back, exposing the fingernails and making them
look longer. If the intestines become bloated with gas,
blood will come out with great force when the corpse is
staked. Some later doctors suggested that so-called vampires suffered from porphyria, a disease which makes the
eyes, skin, and teeth red, and causes cracked skin to bleed
when it comes in contact with sunlight. It is also believed
that to replenish the lost iron in their systems, victims of
porphyria were instructed to drink blood, but there is no
solid proof of that hypothesis.

In the twentieth century, vampirism has moved into the
realm of psychiatry, as in Stoker's *Dracula*. Stoker had
actually done a lot of research into both the folklore and
medical vampirism, and the character of Renfield — a
mental patient who swears his devotion to Dracula and eats
insects for their blood — was modeled on real-life case
studies. Vampirism is defined as the act of ingesting blood
while gaining sexual pleasure from the act, and there have
been many cases involving such patients; ironically, the
majority of the patients are female. The most notorious
case of vampirism — and many psychiatrists would hesi-
tate to use that term in conjunction with the case —
culminated in 1949, when John Haigh was executed for

the "acid-bath murders." Between 1944 and 1949 he had killed nine people and drank a cupful of blood from each before putting the bodies in a vat of sulphuric acid to dissolve them. Of course, real-life instances of vampirism don't involve turning victims into vampires, flying about, and shape-shifting into bats. Those aspects remain solely in the fiction.

Buffy the Vampire Slayer is a welcome addition to the growing legend. The writers on the show follow certain conventions of vampire lore while diverging from others. Joss Whedon's vampires don't fly around and change into bats — they drive cars and have relationships like mortals. But Whedon has created a whole new mythology with these demons, and makes their "lives" and how they affect the lives of others the focal point of the show. Whedon's vampires aren't all faceless monsters, but people who were once victimized themselves.

Most importantly, he has altered the formerly defense-less figure of the young woman into a 5'3" killing machine. But one who has problems of her own. However, her duty is her duty and she must learn to live with the very real fact that each new day could be her last. For, "In every generation there is a Chosen One. . . ."

"SHE IS THE SLAYER":

A SARAH MICHELLE GELLAR BIOGRAPHY

PRECOCIOUS GIRL

Her big break is the stuff of Hollywood legend: She was "discovered" while eating in a New York restaurant with some friends. She was four years old at the time.

Sarah Michelle Gellar was born on April 14, 1977, in New York City. She was a bubbly and intelligent youngster, and her mother must have had a hunch that Sarah was destined for greatness. Little did she know it would happen at such a young age. One day in a restaurant, a woman approached the table where Sarah and some friends of her mother were eating, apparently after she had watched the animated youngster for some time, and asked Sarah if she'd like to be on television. Gellar is slightly embarrassed when she remembers the encounter, recalling that she immediately turned to the agent and proudly rhymed off her full name, phone number, parents' names, and address. "I didn't know what I was doing," she laughs.

She impressed the woman nonetheless, and Sarah returned home and announced to her mother Rosellen that she was going to be on television. Her mother thought the whole thing was a prank, because her daughter didn't have any acting experience — that is, until she received a phone call from the agent setting up Sarah's audition. Rosellen's own curiosity (and probably some pleading on Sarah's part) pushed her to check the situation out. The next day she and Sarah were at Sarah's first audition.

The movie was called *An Invasion of Privacy*, and the cast boasted some notable names. The star was Valerie Harper, and Sarah would audition for the part of her daughter. Other cast members included Carol Kane (from *Taxi*), Jeff Daniels (*Dumb and Dumber*), Robby Benson (*Ice Castles*), and Jerry Orbach (*Law and Order*). The audition was held late in the afternoon, and Sarah was given a scene that she was supposed to read with Valerie Harper, but Harper had already left for the day. The youngster grabbed the script, said it was no problem, and started reading her part. When she came to one of Harper's lines, she'd lower her voice and read it out, imitating Valerie. The casting agents found her irresistible and hired her right then and there.

Word spread quickly about this precocious young lady, and Sarah was soon made the Burger King spokesperson in a series of commercials that aired in 1981. Many years later, when Sarah appeared on *The Tonight Show with Jay Leno* to promote *Buffy the Vampire Slayer*, she laughed that they had to hire a speech coach to help her with her pronunciation when she was doing the commercials. "I couldn't say 'burger.' I kept saying 'buga, buga' " (*Tonight Show*, September 8, 1997). She eventually learned the proper pronunciation, though, and soon North America would be charmed by a little girl in a Burger King restaurant, sitting cross-legged on a chair with long dark pigtails. She was adorable, yet spoke in a very matter-of-fact way that made her seem beyond her years. Audiences everywhere loved her — with one exception.

One of her commercials led to a groundbreaking court case that would forever change the face of competitive advertising. In it, Sarah tells the audience that Burger King

Valerie Harper, Sarah, and Richard Masur in
Invasion of Privacy, Sarah's first acting role.
EVERETT COLLECTION

burgers are bigger than McDonald's hamburgers and that the burgers are flame-broiled rather than fried like they are at McDonald's. This was the first time in television history that a company had used a competitor's name in a critical way. McDonald's sued Burger King, the ad agency who put out the commercials, and Sarah, for slander.

"I was five," she remembers. "I couldn't even say the word 'lawyer' and a few months later I was telling my friends, 'I can't play. I've got to give a deposition' " (qtd. in Pearlman). The lawsuit was settled out of court in 1982, but it did set a precedent whereby companies could now name other companies' products in their advertising. Sarah did 30 spots in total for Burger King, and the fast-food chain followed up her commercials with their now infamous "Where's the Beef?" campaign, clearly implying the burger with no beef was from McDonald's.

Sarah now had a recognizable face and was in demand. *An Invasion of Privacy*, which she had begun filming the week after her first audition, finally aired in 1983. Sarah then appeared in a feature film called *Over the Brooklyn Bridge*, which featured a stellar cast, including Elliott Gould, Margaux Hemingway, Carol Kane, Sid Caesar, and Shelley Winters. After completing these movies, Sarah took a bit of a hiatus from acting in larger productions (she was, after all, only in grade two). During this time, she focused more on her schoolwork and her friends, although she did continue to do commercials.

By 1986, though, she was back in business, appearing as Emily in an episode of *Spenser for Hire*. Sarah loved working with the show's star, Robert Urich: "I was eight or nine, and he was just wonderful to me," she remembers (qtd. in Brady). The same year she appeared in her first theatre production, Horton Foote's *The Widow Claire*. The play was at the Circle in the Square Theatre in New York City, and the cast must have been like a dream for a nine-year-old girl: her co-stars were Matthew Broderick and Eric Stoltz. She remembers that when she was first cast to work with them, they weren't big-name actors, but soon afterward, *Ferris Bueller's Day Off* and *Some Kind of Wonderful*, starring Broderick and Stoltz respectively, were released. "I was the most popular girl in school, because I was working with both of them!" (qtd. in Brady).

That popularity didn't last. When it was time for junior high school, Sarah enrolled in Columbia Preparatory School in New York and she soon realized it would be very difficult for her to fit in. First of all, many of the students came from very wealthy families, and Sarah's mother was a teacher, with a more modest income. "Many students were used to having everything handed to them on a silver platter," Sarah says. "Everything *I* got I worked hard for and got on my own" (qtd. in Collymore). As many children know, kids at a junior-high age can be very cruel, and the students at Columbia Prep were no exception. Sarah became a loner because the other kids wouldn't hang out with her. Probably out of jealousy for Sarah's talent and success, they punished her for being famous by harassing her constantly. Sarah was miserable at school, so she continued putting most of her efforts into her acting.

In 1988, she landed a small role in the Chevy Chase movie *Funny Farm*, in which she played a student. Strangely, her performance went entirely uncredited. In 1989 she appeared in the feature film *High Stakes*, a thriller starring Kathy Bates and Sally Kirkland. Sarah starred as Kirkland's daughter, Karen, and this was the only time she was credited as Sarah Gellar. She found out that there was another actress using that same name, so from then on she used her full name. That same year she hosted *Girl Talk*, a cheesy Saturday-morning TV talk show for young girls, where the hosts would sit and talk about clothes, guys, and other topics that could be considered "girl talk." She co-hosted

Sarah, as she appeared in her grade eight yearbook.

this show with Soleil Moon Frye, best known as Punky Brewster, and Rod Brogan, who went on to *Major Dad* and *One Life To Live*. However, the lighthearted show had a very small viewership, and was soon canceled.

By this time, at the age of 13, Sarah was so busy with everything happening in her life that her mother had her wear a pager so she'd know where her daughter was. Sarah shares a close relationship with her mother. Her parents were divorced when she was very young, and she has always been reluctant to talk about her father, except to say that they don't get along and he is no longer part of her life. However, she has not grown up fatherless. Her mother remarried in the early 1990s, and Sarah says her stepfather has supported her in all of her achievements. "My stepfather always says that when he sees how many things I handle in a day, he'd be willing to hire a young person like me, because now he sees what an incredible thing it is to see kids so focused and how much they have to offer," she says proudly (qtd. in Rush). She has said that she considers him to be more of a father than her biological one.

Sarah always speaks of her mother with tenderness, and it's clear that her mother attended her auditions with her, watched out for her, and kept her grounded. However, she was not a typical stage mother who would make decisions for her daughter. Sarah explains, "My mother is not living vicariously through me. . . . It has always been my choice to act. If at any time I wanted to give it up, she would be behind me 100 percent." She adds, "My mom has always been behind me and we are very close" (qtd. in Collymore).

It was Sarah's mother who realized how unhappy Sarah was at the prep school. Because it was a regular private school, the other students simply couldn't identify with her lifestyle at all. Sarah admits now that she had many of

Sarah with her favorite person in
the world, her mother, Rosellen.
JUDIE BURNSTEIN/GLOBE PHOTOS

the same problems in junior high that Buffy has in high
school, because she was misunderstood. Buffy has to slay
vampires when she should be doing homework or dating,
whereas Sarah faced a similar problem: "I had that same
decision — do I go to a school dance or slumber party or
do I go to an audition?" Her favorite movie of all time is
Heathers — which probably tells a lot about how she
regarded her school years. (In *Heathers*, Winona Ryder
plays a student who doesn't fit in with the rich girls she
hangs out with. In a bizarre twist, Christian Slater's character appears and conspires with her to begin killing their
classmates.) Sarah was made to feel ashamed of her accom-
plishments and was never proud of what she did. "I never
liked to talk about my acting, because if I did I was branded
a snob, and if I didn't I was still a snob. I would cry because
I didn't understand why people didn't like me" (qtd. in
Collymore).

Her mother transferred her to the Professional Children's School in Manhattan. Immediately there was a difference in how Sarah was treated, because the other students worked, just like she did. She made many friends and finally felt as though people understood her. "It's for anyone with irregular schedules — musicians from Juilliard, ballerinas from the School of American Ballet, and writers, and just the most *talented* group of young people where your talent is special, but it doesn't affect your schoolwork" (qtd. in Roesch). At this time, Sarah was acting, going to school, taking figure-skating lessons, and learning tae kwon do. She had studied the martial art for four years, and at the time was two belts away from her black belt, even placing fourth in competition once. "I would get up in the morning, go to the ice rink, then go to school, then go to auditions, then go to tae kwon do. I was cracking" (qtd. in Martinez). Rosellen could see her daughter was overworked, so she told Sarah it was time for her to make a choice — she could do two things at once, but no more. Sarah naturally chose school and acting. (Little did she know how important that tae kwon do would be for her in the future.) Sarah graduated from the school with a 4.0 grade-point average after only two and a half years, but while there her career skyrocketed, setting the stage for the stardom that would soon follow.

FROM SCHOOLGIRL
TO SOAP STAR

In 1991 Sarah was cast in the made-for-TV movie *A Woman Named Jackie*, which was about Jacqueline Bouvier Kennedy Onassis. Sarah played the young Jacqueline Bouvier, while seasoned stage actress Roma Downey played her as an adult. Downey went on to play Hippolyta alongside Lucy Lawless and Kevin Sorbo in *Hercules and the Amazon Women* before landing the lead role in the hugely popular television series *Touched by an Angel*. Sarah loved Downey and recalls that she wanted to be like her. She began mimicking her movements on the set, and Downey was flattered. For the purposes of the movie, Sarah's imitation led to an uncanny similarity in speech and action between the younger and older Jackies, making both performances seem believeable and seamless. Interestingly, one of the cast members was Mark Metcalf, who would later square off against Buffy as The Master.

In 1992, shortly after starting at the new school, Sarah appeared in the premiere cast of the latest Neil Simon play, *Jake's Women*. In it, she played 12-year-old Molly, despite being 15, and it began a pattern in her career where Sarah would often play someone who was either older or younger than herself. A year earlier, she had won the role of Sydney Orion Rutledge in the Fox teen soap opera, *Swans Crossing*, although the episodes didn't air until a full year after the pilot had been filmed. Playing Sydney would definitely help her win her next role in *All My Children*. Sydney is a manipulator, the daughter of the mayor in the tiny seaside town of Swans Crossing. When asked to describe her character, Sarah answered, "Well, Sydney is kind of like the town witch. She doesn't really care about anyone else's feelings and she feels that everything revolves around her, and it usually does. I guess there are always similarities and differences, but I try to keep the bad parts of Sydney out of my life." Ironically, a reviewer for *Entertainment Weekly* would comment, when describing Sydney, "Picture a younger, blonder Erica Kane." The show itself, focusing on the lives of 12 young people, was mediocre at best — it made *Saved by the Bell* look like a high-quality program! The town boasted the Swans Cleaners, Swans

Auto Shop, and Swans Café (which had a phone shaped like a swan), and just made the viewer wonder if anyone in this town could live without swans. Despite the near-ridiculousness of the show, it garnered a small but devoted following of fans. Mira Sorvino even appeared in early episodes (before her Oscar, of course).

Swans Crossing prided itself on standing apart from other shows, especially *Beverly Hills, 90210*, in that it didn't deal with "issues." For Fox, though, the only thing that mattered were the ratings, which were decent, but not stellar. Admittedly, how Fox imagined that a show geared to seven- to 15-year-olds would do well in a 2 PM time slot remains a mystery, but after three months of the daily soap, it was put on hiatus. To see if it could pick up any new fans, the network re-broadcast the first three months of the show — in exactly the same time slot. The series had had a lot of potential among younger viewers, and the producers had even marketed *Swans Crossing* dolls to coincide with the show. However, the ratings weren't high enough to cover the cost of producing a daily show, and the series was canceled.

All was not lost, though, for after *Swans Crossing* was finished, Sarah moved on to an audition that would change her life forever.

Sarah had no idea what part she would be getting when she attended the audition for *All My Children*. She knew it would be for a young person, and she'd probably play someone's child. Then she was cast as the daughter of the manipulative Erica Kane, played by Susan Lucci. Sarah was very nervous the day she walked onto the set. After all, *All My Children* was one of the hottest soap operas on television, and Erica Kane was *the* diva of soap divas. Her fears were quickly assuaged on her first day on the set. Lucci was rehearsing a scene with Michael Nader, who plays Dmitri, but she stopped and came over to welcome Sarah.

She then accompanied the younger actress around the set, introducing her to everyone. Sarah was very touched. "I couldn't have asked to work with anyone better," Sarah told *Daytime TV* at the time. "You can't not have a good working relationship with her." She would soon be singing a different tune.

Sarah's character, Kendall Hart, entered the show's story line just as Erica was about to get married. Sarah often jokes about the plot and what a whirlwind it was, and she's not kidding. From 1993 to 1995 her character went through just about everything. Kendall made her first appearance on *All My Children* on February 24, 1993. Erica had been raped and made pregnant when she was 14, but she'd given the baby up for adoption and tried to forget it had ever happened. Kendall shows up as someone who idolizes Erica, but won't tell her the truth about who she really is. Mona, Erica's mother, sees the birthmark on the back of Kendall's neck that identifies her as Erica's

The *Swans Crossing* cast goofing around at Planet Hollywood, 1992. From left: Kristen Mahon, Brittany Daniel, Stacey Moseley, and Sarah hold Shane McDermott on their laps.

daughter, but it isn't until Bianca, Erica's *other* daughter, is injured in a riding accident that Kendall tells Erica who she really is. When Kendall then becomes obsessed with finding her birth father, Erica forbids it. Kendall convinces Dmitri to help her, and he does. Erica finds out, kicks Kendall out of the house, and leaves Dmitri, saying she wants a divorce. Kendall spends the night with Dmitri's assistant, Anton, and then tells Erica that Dmitri tried to rape her. In a blind rage, Erica returns and stabs Dmitri with a letter opener, remembering when she'd been raped as a teen. (Are you still with me?)

Kendall starts scheming with Del Henry, another guy in town, about writing a tell-all book on Erica Kane. Erica takes the stand in the attempted murder trial and says she didn't mean to stab Dmitri, but had hallucinated that he was Robert Fields, the man who'd raped her. Kendall takes the stand and swears that Dmitri had raped her and that Erica's act was something he'd pushed her to do. However, during the trial she realizes her real father was a monster, she recants her testimony, and is sent to jail for perjury, setting Erica free. Meanwhile Mona kills Fields and later dies in her sleep (after the actress who played her, Frances Heflin, lost a long battle with cancer). Kendall finds out Anton is Dmitri's son and marries him, but later agrees to a divorce. She and Erica come to an understanding before Kendall leaves Pine Valley for Florida, from whence she came. Whew!!

Kendall's life was pretty complicated, but Sarah loved every minute of it (although she once mentioned that she wished Kendall would calm down a bit). Kendall's crazed behavior allowed Sarah to try things she'd never done before. "It was amazing playing a psycho-loony," she said afterward. "I got to attempt suicide. I shot at people. It was *great*" (qtd. in Rochlin). Sarah probably enjoyed being on this show more than her previous work because of

Sarah with Winsor Harmon, who
played Del Henry on *All My Children*.
BURSTEIN-PHOTOREPORTERS/GLOBE PHOTOS

the challenge. The show was on daily, which meant the characters were given a new script every day. She also learned the importance of getting a scene right the first time. "You get a script a day in advance, you rehearse it once or twice, and you get one take, maybe two, and that is it," she explains. "Contrary to popular belief, we did not have cue cards" (qtd. in Martinez).

The fans loved Sarah. As Kendall, she was deliciously evil, yet you really couldn't help but feel sorry for her because she had been abandoned as a child. In 1994, after having been on the show for less than a year, Sarah was nominated for a Daytime Emmy Award for Outstanding Younger Leading Actress in a Daytime Drama Series. She didn't win that year, but it was definitely a thrill for her to have been nominated after such a short time. However, it was also at this time that the rumors began about the relationship between Sarah and Lucci being less than perfect. Lucci had been nominated for Outstanding Lead Actress in a Daytime Drama Series 14 times, but had never won the award. Sarah would later admit, "It wasn't an easy time in my life. . . . We didn't have a perfect working relationship. We, um, weren't going out to lunch" (qtd. in Rochlin).

The tabloids and other papers began reporting that Lucci and Sarah hated one another. To this day Sarah insists that was not the case, that the papers were blowing things out of proportion. She says they worked well together on-screen, but they didn't have a very good personal relationship. Midway through the season, Sarah decided she would be leaving the show to move on to other projects (and, some say, to get away from Lucci). Sarah must have wondered whether or not she'd made the right decision when in 1995 she was again nominated for the Younger Actress Award — and won (the Emmys were held the same evening as her prom night, but Sarah somehow managed to make it to both). Sarah insisted to Lucci that she had never been in competition with her. "I won for scenes I submitted with her. You don't work alone — this was work we did together" (qtd. in Roesch). The very next day, ABC announced officially that Sarah would be leaving the show. This was six months after Sarah had told them, and she was very unhappy about the timing. "It made me look incredibly bad," she recalls. "I was told by ABC that I couldn't announce my leaving until they made an official announcement. . . . The timing was terrible" (qtd. in Pearlman).

Sarah would later remember that in 1993, after a strange comedy called *Buffy the Vampire Slayer* had hit the movie theaters, her makeup person on the set of *All My Children* joked about how much she looked like Kristy Swanson, the actress who played the title role in the movie.

Perhaps Sarah was destined to become her younger, hipper television incarnation.

MAKE WAY FOR
SOME SERIOUS SLAYAGE

When Sarah was on *All My Children* she was happy to be playing a character who was seven years older than she was. She mentioned in an interview how on television it seemed like adults played kids, but never vice versa. "They just don't write for kids anymore. You always have older people playing younger people. . . . There are some very talented teenagers who can do it just as good, if not better, than any adults, but they're not given a fair chance" (qtd. in Rush). Later she would tell *Daytime TV* that she far preferred daytime television to prime time: "I don't mean to bash all these people who leave daytime for prime time, but I don't think those nighttime sitcoms are a hell of a lot better these days. In some cases, daytime has a lot more talented people than in prime time." One wonders if she regrets those earlier comments now. However, she can't really be blamed for making them. After all, she hadn't yet met Joss Whedon.

Whedon launched his career as a writer on *Roseanne*. His grandfather had written scripts for 1950s and '60s television shows like *Mayberry* RFD, *The Donna Reed Show*, and *The Dick Van Dyke Show*, and Whedon's father had written for *Alice* and *Benson* in the '70s and '80s. Whedon's first film was the quirky and weird *Buffy the Vampire Slayer* (which was released when Joss was a mere 27 years old), starring Kristy Swanson as a blond cheerleader who discovers she's been chosen to slay vampires to save the world. Donald Sutherland played her weary watcher, Luke Perry the love interest, and Paul Reubens (a.k.a. Pee-wee Herman) one of the vampires. The movie flopped at the box office, and Whedon chalks it up to the fact that the final product no longer followed his original vision. He'd wanted a dark comedy that looked at the slayer's calling as a metaphor for high school. Instead, it became a more mainstream comedy with most of the action and horror removed.

Whedon's talent as a writer, however, was not overlooked. He became Hollywood's Mr. Fixit and was brought in to jazz up scripts like *Speed*, *Waterworld*, and *Twister*, giving them more colorful dialogue (in all of these movies, his writing went uncredited). Whedon gained more recognition when he co-penned the hilarious and clever *Toy Story*.

At around the same time, *Buffy the Vampire Slayer* was released on home video, and the rental figures were far more encouraging than the box-office receipts had been. The movie was turning into a cult hit, and its producers were taking notice. Fran Rubel Kuzui, the film's director, and Gail Berman, who had thought the movie would make a great television show when she'd first read it, approached Whedon and asked if he'd be interested. He was very interested. As the series' creator, head writer, executive producer, and occasional director, he would finally have the ability to do what he wanted with the series concept. Kuzni, Berman, and Whedon felt that if the show came out five years after the movie, it would avoid direct comparisons to its predecessor, and viewers would recognize the difference between the two. The Warner Brothers network expressed an interest in the project, and auditions began. That same week, Whedon was nominated for an Oscar for *Toy Story*.

When Sarah's agent contacted her about a new show about high school kids battling real demons, she was excited about the concept and decided she had to play the part of Buffy. After all, she could do comedy, drama — and tae kwon do. When she arrived at the auditions, however, the casting agents saw her long dark hair and pale skin and asked her to read for a different role. They said she would be perfect as the snobby and dominating Cordelia, especially after having done such a convincing job in the similar role of Kendall. Sarah went through the audition, but pleaded with the casting agents to let her try for Buffy. They finally relented.

Whedon remembers the experience. Sarah walked in and immediately seemed to possess all the qualities he wanted for Buffy — she had to be funny, tough, attractive, and weird. Now he had to see how her reading went. He was not disappointed. "She gave us a reading that was letter perfect," Whedon recalls, "and then said, 'By the way, it doesn't say this on my résumé but I did take tae kwon do for four years and I'm a brown belt. Is that good?' No, perfect," Joss thought to himself (qtd. in Kutzera). He says she nailed the part right then and there, but Sarah has a different recollection of events. "It was the most awful experience of my life, but I was so driven," she recalls. After the initial audition, she went through five more auditions, and five screen tests! But she prevailed, and the part was hers. She packed her things and moved to Los Angeles. The pilot episode was shot and the WB was convinced — this would be a very big show.

However, *Buffy the Vampire Slayer* would not have a fall premiere, but would be added as a mid-season replacement in case another show didn't fare very well. Having a mid-season premiere gave Joss and the others more time to prepare. It also gave the actors more time to get to know one another. The members of the ensemble cast were mostly new to the business, with the exceptions of Sarah and Anthony Stewart Head, but they clicked right away.

Nobody knew if the show would be picked up for a second season, so the cast gave it their all in an attempt to win over the audience and the WB. Joss wrote the 11 episodes as one long story arc, and the final show of the season, "Prophecy Girl," had a completeness about it, so viewers would know that the characters were going to be okay, even if they never returned. However, he intentionally left some holes where it would be very easy to start the show up again if it was renewed.

The ensemble immediately had an on-screen chemistry, as is evident in the first episodes. Xander and Willow seem like old friends, and if we do sense moments of discomfort on Willow's part, it can be attributed to the crush she's got on Xander. Cordelia is wonderfully snobbish, and Xander is the wisecracker. Buffy has a sardonic wit about her, yet is vulnerable in certain situations, and Giles is the stuttery librarian who seems bewildered that his charge would rather date guys than slay vampires. Angel is brooding and mysterious, and there is a tense chemistry between him and Buffy. The cast was perfect, and they were all delighted to be working with Joss, leading him to joke, "I don't think they fear me nearly enough."

Sarah loved her new character, despite having problems with some of the dialogue. She told *Rolling Stone* magazine,

"I still have to ask Joss, 'What does this mean?' because I don't speak the lingo. I think he makes it up half the time." (Joss admits that he does.) *Buffy the Vampire Slayer* was different from all the other high school shows because of its focus on a single, tough young woman. The mid-1990s saw a wave of empowered women on television: Peta Wilson's character on *La Femme Nikita* is a deadly assassin; *Xena: Warrior Princess* featured two women, Xena and Gabrielle, who have changed the face (and gender) of action shows; and *The X-Files* introduced Dana Scully, an intelligent and brave woman who must fight powers much bigger than herself and stand up for her own beliefs. However, all of these female characters had made it past their adolescence, whereas Buffy was still battling her way through high school *besides* having to take on vampires. "She doesn't know if she wants to be a cheerleader or fight vampires," Sarah says of Buffy, "and that is what makes her interesting and believable. Buffy is a person who is lost, who doesn't know where she belongs — and you feel for her" (qtd. in Kutzera). To make her character even more realistic, Sarah took up kick-boxing, street fighting, boxing, and gymnastic training.

Whedon knew he'd made the right choice with Sarah, and he refers to her as "like the best actress ever" (qtd. in Persons). He was delighted to see how she pulled off the role and how she was everything the movie Buffy wasn't. "Even though she's a vampire slayer," he says, "she still makes you feel everything she goes through, and that's not easy." He adds, "She is also great at pouting."

As the filming for season one continued, Joss knew his original vision was being restored. He stressed that his show was not about "issues," like most teen shows, but that the subjects — no matter how many vampires or demons are lurking about — would be culled from the real fears of teenagers. Sarah agrees: "The scariest horror exists in reality," she told the *New York Daily News*. "It's feeling invisible, date rape — these are situations teenagers understand and can relate to because it's happening to them."

When people ask Whedon why the townspeople of Sunnydale don't question the strange goings-on, he says that his series operates under the same principle of disbelief that shows like *Superman* had. In *Superman*, people saw a man flying around in red tights and they just accepted he was there, just as the citizens of Sunnydale rationalize the vampire activity. Anthony Stewart Head remarked that he loves Whedon's unpredictable writing style, and joked that the cast has a constant fear of who will go next. "I thought it was wonderful last season when he bumped off the principal," he said recently. "At that moment, you knew there weren't any lines he wouldn't cross, and anything goes" (qtd. in Ferrante).

Head wasn't the only person who admired Whedon's work. When the show finally premiered on March 10, 1997, it garnered a Nielsen rating of 3.4, meaning approximately 3,298,000 households were watching. It was one of the biggest ratings in WB history. Whedon attributes the show's initial success to the huge ad campaign the WB had launched to promote it. As the series continued, it became the biggest show on the network. And it wasn't just the fans who were loving it — it was a critical smash. Daniel Fienberg of the *Daily Pennsylvanian* raved, "Less cheesy than nearly every show on Fox, and edgier than every teen show that ABC, NBC, and CBS have put out in years, *Buffy* is (to create a TV Guide cover blurb) 'The Best Show On TV That You Would Make Fun Of If You Didn't Know Better.'" Joe Queenan of TV Guide wrote that *Buffy the Vampire Slayer*, "far from being the stuff of fantasy or mere over-the-top satire, is the most realistic portrayal of contemporary teenage life on television today." Tom Carson of the *Village*

Voice agreed, writing, "I can't think of a TV show that better captures how adolescence feels. . . ." He added that "the show's clear-eyed recognition that autonomy can be one hard row to hoe . . . puts it miles ahead of upbeat ads about girl Little Leaguers." Scott D. Pierce of *Deseret News* claimed, *"Buffy the Vampire Slayer* is the coolest show on TV." Thomas Hine of the *New York Times* called Buffy "television's most stylish female hand-to-hand fighter since Diana Rigg played Emma Peel on *The Avengers* three decades ago." He commented, "Being a teenager used to be the stuff of comedies. Now it's a horror show." Canadian Mark Kingwell, writing for *Saturday Night*, said that Buffy is "a true 1990s TV heroine" and "Gellar's edgy performances are a pleasure to watch." And last (possibly least), even Howard Stern told Sarah Michelle Gellar, "Your acting in this is perfect." He added, "It's one of the best hours on television."

Joss Whedon and company had a hit on their hands.

THE NEW SCREAM QUEEN

Oddly enough, after months of anticipating how television audiences would react to *Buffy the Vampire Slayer*, Sarah wasn't actually in Los Angeles to witness the huge promotional campaign the WB launched. When the show went on a five-month hiatus between the first and second seasons, Sarah found a side career as a horror-movie scream queen for wunderkind screenwriter Kevin Williamson.

Williamson can be credited single-handedly with reviving the horror genre for the '90s, despite having been told by a high school English teacher that he'd never succeed as a writer. He attended theater school on an acting scholarship, but was more interested in writing the scripts than acting them out. His first script, *Killing Mrs. Tingle*, was bought as a film option, but failed to make it to the big screen. He returned to more well-known Hollywood jobs like temping and dog walking, but recalls a very strange experience that happened when he was home alone one night. A noise in the kitchen prompted him to grab a butcher knife and a cell phone and call a friend, who began asking him trivia questions about 1980s horror flicks. This surreal situation became the opening scene for a new script, which he penned in three days.

Scream was bought by Miramax, and became the biggest-grossing horror movie of all time. Starring Neve Campbell, Skeet Ulrich, Courteney Cox, and Drew Barrymore, the movie was an ironic look at the horror-movie genre, poking fun at its conventions while following them at every turn. Fans and critics loved it. Williamson's characters were different — smarter — than their counterparts in earlier horror films, and he is very conscious of how he writes dialogue for his teenage characters. He refers to the teenager of the '90s as "a very self-aware, pop-culture-referenced individual who grew up next to Blockbuster in the self-help, psychobabble '80s" (qtd. in Krantz). His characters don't get scared as easily as victims in earlier horror films; for example, when the killer calls her house and says he's standing on the porch, Sidney (Campbell) throws the front door open to prove him wrong. With a cutting-edge writing style and at only 32 years old, Williamson was very similar to Whedon. It was probably inevitable that he would choose Sarah Michelle Gellar to be one of his stars.

I Know What You Did Last Summer starred Freddie Prinze Jr., Jennifer Love Hewitt, Ryan Phillippe, and Sarah. When Sarah had first read the script, she was a little wary about the role of Helen Shivers, the local beauty queen, because she disliked the idea of playing a dumb blonde. However, after thinking about the character for a while Sarah realized there was more to Helen than she'd originally thought, and she accepted the part. Williamson immediately took to her the same way Whedon had. "You know that when you hire her to do a job she's not going to be in the trailer, complaining about everything," said Williamson. "She's going to be right out there at three in the morning, barefoot, in the freezing cold, giving you the tenth take" (qtd. in Rochlin). Sarah relocated to North Carolina for the duration of filming the movie, and realized how much easier feature films were than television series. On *Buffy*, she worked long hours, and a one-hour episode was filmed over eight days. However, the two-hour movie was shot over two months, so there was ample time to go back and change things. Helen Shivers was an exciting part for her because she was a big fan of horror films, having seen all the *Friday the 13th* and *Halloween* movies. "There's nothing like the adrenaline rush you get," Sarah says of horror films. "You know it's fake, that nothing bad is actually gonna happen, but it's still scary and fun. It's kind of like a roller-coaster ride" (qtd. in Graham and Wolf).

I Know What You Did Last Summer was an adaptation of a Lois Duncan novel of the same name. Four teenagers are out spending a frolicky evening on the beach. On the way home they hit a person standing in the road. Desperate, and assuming the police will accuse them of drunk driving, they take the body and dump it in a lake. However, their problems don't disappear. The honors student can now barely get passing grades. The promising football player falls apart and quits the team. The beauty queen gets stuck working at a clothing store, haunted by the past. And the past catches up to them when they begin receiving mysterious notes which read, "I know what you did last summer."

The movie, while not as clever or deep as *Scream*, is filled with suspense and gore. The killer dresses as a fisherman and guts his victims with a huge meat hook. At one point, he chases Helen through the streets to her sister's clothing store, where she pounds on the glass begging to get in. Her sister nonchalantly wanders away to get the keys, and the suspense created by Gellar pounding her fists on the window is heartstopping. Filming this scene, however, was difficult for Sarah because she had been conditioned over the previous months to fight back. Instead of running, Sarah kept turning to fight the killer. "I'd punch the guy, and it'd be like a right hook to the jaw — boom!" she laughs. "And Jim's [director Jim Gillespie] like, 'No, you flail your arms' " (qtd. in Roesch). She would continue to fight later when she was working on *Scream 2*, and Wes Craven, the horror legend and director of that film, would joke to her, "Don't kill the bad man, because then he can't come back for a sequel" ("Q&A with Sarah Michelle Gellar").

Freddie Prinze Jr., Sarah, Jennifer Love Hewitt,
and Ryan Phillippe in Kevin Williamson's
I Know What You Did Last Summer.
EVERETT COLLECTION

So Sarah learned to run from the killers, but that quickly posed another problem. She appeared to be too athletic for a beauty queen and kept outrunning the bad guys to the point where they couldn't keep up. So the director put her in six-inch heels, and Sarah put pebbles in her shoes, and she slowed right down. Once she got used to being helpless, Sarah enjoyed the challenge of playing someone so different from Buffy. "I don't think that Helen — I hope — doesn't really have any Buffy traits. I hope I did a good enough departure that you don't sit there and think, 'Oh, there's Buffy' " (qtd. in Roesch).

Sarah enjoyed working on the film because she became very close to her co-stars. Considering that everything in Southport, North Carolina, closed at 9 PM, there was really nothing else to do. She and Hewitt would wander around the town occasionally, but it became a frightening activity as filming went on, because every time they saw a fisherman in his rain gear they'd jump in fright. The other disadvantage to filming in Southport was that the towns-people were unhappy that a group of film people were shaking up their town, and began to resent their presence.

To this day Sarah is in touch with Freddie Prinze, Jr. who has become one of her closest friends. She also had great admiration for Ryan Phillippe, saying, "He's such an amazing actor that there were times we'd be filming and I'd be so distracted by what he was saying" (qtd. in Graham and Wolf).

Meanwhile, back in the civilized world (i.e., cities with cable), *Buffy* was becoming a hit and Sarah didn't know it. Web sites devoted to the show and its stars were popping up on the Internet, and by the end of the first season, there were over 40 of them. *Buffy* posters were in subways, on billboards, and on the sides of buses, but isolated in South-port, Sarah had no idea. She got a clue, though, when she visited New York during a downpour and people still recognized her. "I have mascara running down my face, and people are going by in cars honking their car horns, going, 'Hey, Buffy.' I couldn't believe it" (qtd. in Thompson).

On its opening weekend, *I Know What You Did Last Summer* grossed $16 million, almost recouping its budget of $17 million. Throughout its long six-month run, the movie grossed over $70 million worldwide.

Partway through filming *I Know What You Did Last Summer*, Williamson offered Sarah a small part in his next big film, *Scream 2*. Many young actors in Hollywood had been hankering for a role in a Williamson film, so to be offered a part in two was very flattering for Sarah. Before she began filming *I Know What You Did Last Summer*, Sarah had never actually seen *Scream*, so she went and watched it in the theater: "I saw it with Charisma Carpenter and Alyson Hannigan from *Buffy* and we were so loud the people next to us asked for their money back because they said we were disrupting their movie-watching experience" ("Q&A with Sarah Michelle Gellar"). To film *Scream 2*, Sarah again relocated, this time to Atlanta. She says she was a little intimidated at first when she realized the sequel would once again star Neve Campbell, because the cast of *Buffy the Vampire Slayer* watched *Party of Five* religiously. However, as she got into an elevator with the cast of *Scream 2*, Neve turned to Sarah and said that Jennifer Love Hewitt wanted her to say hey. Sarah knew everything would be fine. In fact, when she realized who the rest of the ensemble cast were, she described working on the movie as being like a high school reunion, having attended high school with Jerry O'Connell and Rebecca Gayheart.

Sarah's role in *Scream 2* is actually very small, but it was convenient for her because she had to get back to California to begin filming the second season of *Buffy the Vampire Slayer*. In the movie she plays a sorority sister who gets a phone call from the killer when she's alone in the sorority

Cici Cooper (Sarah) gets attacked at her
sorority house in Wes Craven's *Scream 2.*
EVERETT COLLECTION

house, being "sober sister" for the evening. Williamson had
gotten used to Sarah's sense of humor and sarcasm when
she was on the set of *I Know What You Did Last Summer*, so
he'd written this part especially for her. Sarah's brief time
on screen is great and full of suspense. Williamson was on
the set to watch her final scene, and Sarah laughs, "When
he saw me on the set of *Scream 2*, he said he just loves the
way I die" (qtd. in Hobson). *Scream 2* was a fascinating
experience for Sarah, because she worked for the first time
with Wes Craven, who had directed the *Nightmare on Elm
Street* films. She gained a profound admiration for how he
directed. "Whereas most movies have some guy off camera
going 'bang' to make you turn around," she explains, "Wes
hides people in different places just to freak you out. And
it works" ("Q&A with Sarah Michelle Gellar"). *Scream 2*
had a dark comic edge to it that *I Know What You Did Last
Summer* lacked, so it was more up Sarah's alley. She was

thrilled to do both movies because of the diversity of the characters, and because "they offered me the opportunity to do drama, to do horror, to do action, to do comedy. That's an actor's dream" (qtd. in Wolf). No wonder she enjoys being on *Buffy the Vampire Slayer* so much.

Scream 2 garnered $33 million on its opening weekend, the biggest opening of any Miramax film and the biggest December opening of any movie in history. It grossed $96 million in its first month alone and was re-released into theatres April 26, 1998, raking in another $50 million worldwide. Sarah had just finished filming two of the most successful horror films in history, and when she returned to LA she realized she was also starring in a very successful television show. She was on a roll.

TELEVISION'S HOTTEST GRRL

Following the popularity of the first season of *Buffy the Vampire Slayer*, the WB network allowed Whedon to write deeper situations into the series, develop the characters, alter their relationships, and tighten the ensemble cast into one of the strongest on television. The season premiere featured an angry, depressed, and confused Buffy, setting the stage for a season that would delve into the characters' personal relationships and have more continuity from episode to episode than in season one. The problems that teenagers have in high school would also be handled more seriously than in the first season. Because of the show's strong female following, Buffy's strength and intelligence were made more prominent as well. "The problem with most high schools is they don't stress individuality," says Sarah. "*Buffy* shows girls it's okay to be different" (qtd. in Martinez).

The new formula worked, and the ratings climbed steadily. Viewers tuned in week after week to watch the development of the relationship between Buffy and Angel, and the stars of the show were becoming recognizable faces. Sarah had become one of the hottest young stars in the world with both her movies and her hit television show. She was living proof that Hollywood was finally starting to write realistic parts for people her age, rather than making them caricatures. "What Kevin did with his scripts, and what Joss has done for me with Buffy," she said, "is written three-dimensional human beings: people who make mistakes, good choices, bad choices, have flaws" (qtd. in Roesch). Talk shows began scrambling to get the stars on, and suddenly everyone was in demand.

Fame has its disadvantages, however. Sarah was used to doing many things at once, but she was busier now than she'd ever been. She began filming the second season of *Buffy* while finishing work on *Scream 2*, and then hit the talk show circuit and had newspaper and television interviews. One of her favorite stories, which she related in several interviews, was that one morning she was driving to the set with the top down on her convertible and she noticed a lot of people staring at her. Assuming that people were recognizing who she was, she thought nothing of it. However, the stares got weirder and weirder until she glanced down and realized she was wearing nothing but a slip — she had been so tired she'd forgotten to put her dress on! She knew then that she would have to start getting more sleep, but she takes it all in stride: "Yeah, I don't have much of a life beyond work, but how many other girls get to really release their inner demons for a living?" (qtd. in Pearlman).

On January 17, 1998, Sarah hosted *Saturday Night Live*. Although the show had been waning for a few seasons, with falling ratings, lame skits, and a lot of criticism, this episode was very funny. Even Rosie O'Donnell later said to Sarah of the show, "I think it was the funniest one this season." Sarah admitted to being extemely nervous beforehand, and she'd thought to herself, "I'm gonna be the first host to just get out there and go, 'Uh . . . uh. . . .'" However, Rosie was right. Sarah brought her sarcasm to many of the scenes, making otherwise flat skits absolutely hilarious. In a spoof of *Buffy the Vampire Slayer* taking over the time slot left open by *Seinfeld*, Sarah executed a perfect impression of Julia Louis-Dreyfuss as Elaine. In another skit, called "Goth Talk," she played a goth who hosts her own cable access show and is trying to cover up a dark past as a fan of cheesy pop music.

Right after Sarah was on *Saturday Night Live*, the *Buffy* ratings passed the four-million mark, and two weeks later it had surpassed five million. The show was huge. To top it all off, the show won three Petcabus awards, which are given out to underappreciated shows that deserve awards. *Buffy the Vampire Slayer* won the Golden Petcabus, given to the best underappreciated show on television, as well as awards for Best Ensemble Cast and Best Recurring Character (Juliet Landau for Drusilla). On March 10, 1998, Sarah herself won a Blockbuster Award for Favorite Supporting Actress in a Horror Movie for *I Know What You Did Last Summer*.

The future is bright for Sarah Michelle Gellar. She stars in *Cruel Intentions*, a modernized version of *Les Liaisons Dangereuses*, co-starring Ryan Phillippe, and *Vanilla Fog*, where she plays a woman believed to possess magical powers. She is also featured in the computer-animated film *Small Soldiers*, as the voice of one of the Gwendy dolls.

Sarah has proven that she's not a child star but a serious actress. She has starred in successful movies and in one of the hottest shows on television today. Is she in danger of being typecast? It's not likely, because in the past she has chosen roles that were very diverse. But as Sarah puts it, so what if she is? "If this is typecasting, you know, God help me, I guess. . . . I should be so lucky" ("Listen Up with Sarah Michelle Gellar").

What we can bank on is that Sarah will always be a busy person, taking on a million tasks at once with detailed precision. But that's okay with her. As she told *Rolling Stone* magazine, "If you want something done, ask a busy person to do it. That's going to be my epitaph."

THE REST OF THE GANG

THE *BUFFY THE VAMPIRE SLAYER* CO-STARS

The most daring aspect of Buffy the Vampire Slayer *isn't the writing, the directing, or the underlying metaphors in each episode: it is Joss Whedon's choice of an ensemble cast. With the exception of Sarah Michelle Gellar and Anthony Stewart Head, the members of the Buffy cast have had very little experience and are fresh faces on television. Perhaps it is for that very reason that they work so well — the audience can't associate them with any other characters. What follows are brief biographical descriptions of the major cast members.*

ANTHONY STEWART HEAD
(RUPERT GILES)

Though he may not be immediately recognizable to a North American audience, Anthony Stewart Head has an enormous acting portfolio, ranging from movies to commercials. Born on February 20, 1954, in Camden, England, Anthony Stewart Head is nothing like his stuffy television counterpart, Rupert Giles. He has worked in movies, television, and theater, although most people identify him as the Taster's Choice guy. From 1990 to 1997 there ran a series of commercials in England for Nescafé Gold Blend and in the United States for Taster's Choice, in which a veritable soap opera unfolded. An attractive woman crosses the hall to ask her neighbor for some coffee and finds a handsome English gentleman — Tony. A love story evolves over their coffee mugs, and viewers see a son show up and an ex-husband unearthed. Ah, the woes of coffee drinkers. The commercials were huge for the company, and within months of their airing in the United States, sales of Taster's Choice coffee had increased by 10 percent. And they say looks don't sell coffee.

Anthony Stewart Head
FITZROY BARRETT/GLOBE PHOTOS

Tony's career has had far more illustrious moments,
though. On stage he appeared (as Anthony Head) in,
among others, *Godspell*, *Henry V*, *Rosencrantz and Guilden-
stern Are Dead*, *Chess*, *Lady Windermere's Fan*, *Julius Caesar*, and
The Rocky Horror Picture Show. This latter is a favorite role
among fans, and several followers of the cult hit have said
Tony was the best Frank N. Furter ever. Well, he was
without a doubt the sexiest. In a long wig, tons of makeup,
and fishnet stockings, Tony strutted across the stage, singing "Sweet Transvestite" and "I Can Make You a Man"
to the delight of the audience (you can hear .wav and

RealAudio files of him singing "Sweet Transvestite" on the Internet — what a voice!). Tony's singing skills run in the family — his brother, Murray Head, had a hit in 1984 with "One Night in Bangkok."

It was during the run of this show that Tony, believe it or not, perfected some of the more subtle aspects of his acting that he now uses on *Buffy the Vampire Slayer*. If you've seen the show live, you know it is a very interactive production. When Frank N. Furter — the mad, gay scientist — struts out onstage, you shout at him when he sings, heckle him when he talks, and sometimes the rowdier audience members throw things (although that behavior is usually saved for watching the movie). Frank, in return, must insult the audience right back. Tony laughs that he had to learn a whole crop of insults when he was rehearsing the part, and he refused to let any heckling go unanswered. "The show ran for hours because I answered everything!" he says. "After that, they said to me, 'Tony, you have to let some of them go.' So I developed 'the look.' With it I could put down a heckler at the back of a balcony. It was so empowering" (qtd. in Boris).

Tony starred in various BBC television movies, and was in the films *Lady Chatterley's Lover*, *Prayer for the Dying*, and the American-made *Royce*. In 1992 he moved to the United States to appear in television series, and his first was a guest appearance in *Highlander: The Series* in the particularly violent episode "Nowhere to Run." Then he was offered the role of Oliver Sampson on the sci-fi television series, *VR5*. A woman discovers she has powers to access the subconscious of other people through virtual reality. She moves through the various levels of virtual reality on her way to level 5, where she can alter a person's behavior and other events. Sampson is the head of The Committee, a mysterious organization that hires the woman to carry out dangerous assignments that use her ability for questionable purposes. The part of the villain was an unusual one for Tony to play, although he had done it before in movies and television roles. *VR5* lasted only one season, but he then made appearances in an episode of NYPD *Blue*, which is one of the first times he was credited as Anthony Stewart Head.

He noticed that there was a difference between American and British styles of acting. "In the UK, the way of coaching, for the most part, is a bit more stylized, more technical" (qtd. in Persons). In the United States, he says, it's more realistic, and he now prefers a more method style of acting — like rolling on the floor to indicate he'd been in a fight rather than having the makeup people simulate it. He laughs, "Alyson [Hannigan] still won't let me live down the time she tried to pick a bit of fluff off my jacket and I snapped at her, 'Don't touch that! I spent an hour getting that just right!' " (qtd. in Boris).

In 1997 he was offered the role of Rupert Giles in the offbeat *Buffy the Vampire Slayer*. It didn't take long for him to realize this was a part he had to play. "When I read the script I just laughed out loud and I thought, this has to be something," he recalls. "I loved the concept. English people are often always cast as either the bad guy or the stupid stiff-upper-lip guy. This was just so different" (qtd. in Boris). He loves the way Giles just "bumbles through life," and despite all his knowledge, Giles often looks like a deer caught in the headlights when it comes to difficult situations. The *Buffy* cast love the way Tony is so non-Giles when he's off the set, and the online *Buffy* drinking game commands players to chug whenever they spot the earring hole (which is usually well hidden by makeup) in Giles's left ear. Tony splits his time between Los Angeles and his home in Somerset, England, which he shares with his longtime companion, Sarah, and their two daughters, Emily Rose and Daisy May.

Tony has his own official fan club, which is now taking new members. To join the Anthony Stewart Head Fan Club, send $18 (in US funds) to:

Sonja Isaacs — ASHFC
10725 20th Ave NE
Seattle, WA 98125

Include an e-mail address if you have one. If you are online, you can e-mail Sonja at gaspers@eskimo.com to request an application. When you join, you will receive the fan-club newsletter and an autographed picture of Tony, you will be able to send in questions to Tony that will be answered in the newsletter, you will be in touch with other Anthony Stewart Head fans worldwide, and you will be updated on the latest Anthony Stewart Head contests (for which Tony provides signed prizes). Do not send fan mail to Tony at the fan club; all fan mail should be directed to the address at the end of this section.

ALYSON HANNIGAN
(WILLOW ROSENBERG)

Although her résumé isn't as extensive as that of Sarah Michelle Gellar, Alyson Hannigan started acting at the same age as Sarah. Alyson was born in Washington, DC, on March 24, 1974, but she grew up in Atlanta, Georgia. Her parents were photographers, and when they needed a baby in a photo they used her. "When I got old enough where I knew what I was doing," Alyson remembers, "my mom asked me if I wanted to try doing commercials, and I said, 'Yeah!'" (qtd. in Sloane). Alyson was only four years old at the time, but she enjoyed making commercials for companies like Six Flags and Oreos so much that she focused on television full-time. Since then she has had several television roles, appearing on *Picket Fences*, *Touched by an Angel*, *Almost Home*, *The Torkelsons*, and *Roseanne*.

Alyson's big break came in 1988, when she appeared with Seth Green in the Dan Ackroyd film *My Stepmother Is an Alien*, and eventually landed the part of Willow Rosenberg on *Buffy*. Alyson had first heard about the role when a friend of hers mentioned she would be perfect for it. "My agent had a breakdown that he read to me and I think it

Alyson Hannigan at a film premiere.
FITZROY BARRETT/GLOBE PHOTOS

said something like, 'She's a shy wallflower who's still wearing the dress that her mother picked out for her'" (qtd. in Sloane). However, at first she couldn't even get an audition, much less the part. The role of Willow was given to another actress, who filmed the 30-minute presentation that was used to sell the show to the WB network. After the show was picked up, though, the producers decided to recast the part of Willow. It was then that Alyson was called in.

In the same way Sarah recalled her auditions, Alyson remembers that she had 10 of them, and that finally it was down to her and one other actress from New Zealand. In the final audition she had to read with Nick Brendon and Sarah Michelle Gellar, because the real test was to see how she interacted with them. She remembers the audition with a certain amount of horror; she completely messed up because she couldn't pronounce the computer terms in it, and she was convinced the other actress would get the role. Joss told her that although she'd messed up the dialogue, she had a chemistry that the other actress didn't. She was offered the role a few days later.

After filming had begun on the first season, Alyson felt a little out of place because the other actors had become friends over the summer, while she was new to the show. She quickly made friends with Sarah and Nick, though, and was delighted that the chemistry of the cast was so perfect. She insists that she's very different from her character — she wouldn't know how to hack into a computer system if her life depended on it — but that she and Willow have the same sense of humor.

Whedon has never regretted casting the part of Willow: "She treats Willow's lifelong love for Xander as a smoldering passion that she knows will never reach fruition. Another actress might make it a little more obvious, but Alyson's underplaying is just perfect" (qtd. in Persons).

Willow fits in with the other characters in that she isn't part of the popular crowd, but her inherent shyness sets her apart from Xander and Buffy. And Alyson conveys this shyness perfectly. "I wanted Willow to have that kind of insanely colorful interior life that truly shy people often have," Joss explains. "And Alyson has that. She definitely has a loopiness that I found creeping into the way Willow talked, which was great. To an extent, all of the actors conform to the way I write the character, but it really stands out in Willow's case."

DAVID BOREANAZ
(ANGEL)

David Boreanaz was born on May 16, 1971, in Buffalo, New York, to David and Patty Boreanaz. His father is now a well-known weathercaster in Philadelphia, and his mother works at a travel agency. David grew up with two sisters and in high school decided to become a professional football player. Despite his expertise on the football field, a knee injury forced him to drop that career goal and set his sights elsewhere. What the other players didn't know was that David had harbored a secret love of theater ever since his parents had taken him to a production of *The King and I*, starring Yul Brynner, when he was only eight years old. "I was third-row, and I was just blown away by his performance," he remembers. "And I came out and I just knew I wanted to be the King, I wanted to be an actor" (*"Buffy the Vampire Slayer*'s David Boreanaz"). David attended Ithaca College in New York, and while there he decided he would try his hand at acting. Upon graduation he moved to Hollywood, taking odd jobs like valet parking and house painting while getting cast in commercials. Years later, on

David, as he appeared in his senior-year high school yearbook.
SETH POPPEL YEARBOOK ARCHIVES

the *Keenan Ivory Wayans Show*, he admitted that as a valet parker, he would pull away in the car very calmly, but in the garage he and the other valets would drag-race the cars, clocking each other to see how fast they could go.

The only break he got before landing the role of Angel was playing Kelly Bundy's boyfriend in a 1993 episode of *Married . . . With Children*. Over three years went by, during which David turned to theater. One day while David was playing with his dog, Bertha Blue, he was approached by a

Hollywood manager who asked if he was an actor. When David replied that he was, the manager said he knew the perfect role for him. And the rest is history.

His best friend is Nicholas Brendon, but he loves working with the other cast members on *Buffy* as well. He and Sarah Michelle Gellar share a friendship off-screen as well as on, and he jokes, "Before doing kissing scenes, we try to gross each other out by eating things like goldfish crackers or tuna fish" (qtd. in Malkin). He doesn't mind the vampire mask that he wears on the show, even though it takes 80 minutes to put on and another 40 to take off. He says it's just like a normal mask that goes onto your face, "but what they do is then they paint the face on, they use the makeup to blend in. So it's the blending of the makeup that takes so much time. . . . And then you just put the contact lenses on, and then you put the teeth in, and you're ready to rock and roll" (*"Buffy the Vampire Slayer*'s David Boreanaz").

His parents are very proud of him, and David appreciates the support they give him. "One of the best things that could happen is . . . seeing your parents be very proud. I mean, that's a blessing. I'm very fortunate to have such a great family" (*Regis and Kathie Lee*).

David reads all of his fan mail and answers a lot of it as well — he's even been known to call fans on the telephone and surprise them. He says he likes intelligent women: "I like girls who I can have a real conversation with about music, poetry, and great books" (qtd. in Malkin). However, if you have aspirations of being the next woman in David's life, you're a little late. David is happily married to a woman named Ingrid, although he tends to keep his family life private. Mostly he's just overwhelmed that he was lucky enough to have landed this role. "I'm blessed with doing *Buffy*," he says. "I just have to count those blessings and work hard" (qtd. in Malkin).

CHARISMA CARPENTER
(CORDELIA CHASE)

Born on July 23, 1970, Charisma Carpenter says she got her name from a "tacky bottle of Avon perfume from the 1970s" ("Charisma Carpenter Star Chat"). She grew up in Las Vegas, Nevada, in a strict household which her friends dubbed "Alcatraz," but she laughs that she found lots of ways to get in trouble with her parents. "I snuck

Charisma Carpenter at the L.A.
premiere of *Alien Resurrection*.
FITZROY BARRETT/GLOBE PHOTOS

out when they were sleeping to go out with my friends because my parents were very, very strict" ("Q&A with Charisma Carpenter"). However, there was a lot of love in her family, and when asked what her life goals are, Charisma always answers first that she wants to get married and have a family.

Unlike her snobby character on television, Charisma comes across as sweet and charming in print interviews and on television. On *The Keenan Ivory Wayans Show* she burst into a fit of laughter when she remembered that as a child she was part of the Young Entertainers, a group that would go to lodges and perform inspirational songs (let's hope one of them wasn't "The Greatest Love of All"). She was also a child model, appearing in beauty pageants, but she insists her parents weren't like most beauty-pageant parents, and they always gave her the option to quit if she didn't like doing it. In high school Charisma became a cheerleader, enjoying it so much that she became a professional cheerleader for the San Diego Chargers in 1991.

During her teen years she worked in a video store, as a waitress, and as an aerobics instructor, but she decided to try out acting by appearing in commercials, most notably one for Secret antiperspirant. She moved to Los Angeles, but her first impression was not a good one — it was during the LA riots. "The day I came, there was all this outbreak and mayhem and there was a curfew and there was no food in the apartment. So I had to go to this store and when I go out of the apartment complex I turn the corner and there's like cars on fire, people running with sawed-off shotguns and looting," she told Keenan Ivory Wayans. "I was so scared, so I put the car in reverse, got back into the garage, and ate canned soup."

After appearing in a few commercials, she was, not surprisingly, noticed right away and was offered guest-starring roles on *Baywatch* and *Pacific Blue*. Those parts led to her winning the role of Ashley Green on Fox's short-lived Aaron Spelling production *Malibu Shores*. When she auditioned for the role of Cordelia Chase on *Buffy the Vampire Slayer* she had had little experience, but now fans can't imagine anyone but Charisma as Cordelia. She had the part down pat from the first episode, yet was able to develop her character into someone who is caring while still being self-centered. She says she loves Cordy's truthfulness and the way she speaks her mind, but insists she's nothing like her.

Unlike other actors who feel they have to work all the time, Charisma spends a lot of time perfecting things. She isn't interested in filling up all her free time with movies and keeping her plate full, but she doesn't have a lot of free time, anyway. While working on *Buffy*, she says, "I stay up writing my lines over and over again to memorize them so they come across naturally" ("Charisma Carpenter Star Chat"). She's thrilled with all the attention Sarah gets, and says she's not jealous at all, admitting that she hasn't been in the business nearly as long as Sarah. In fact, she says that because she gets less fan mail she's able to respond to all of it. But she's confident the spotlight will be hers one day. "I believe in myself, and it's going to happen when it happens and not any sooner."

NICHOLAS BRENDON
(XANDER HARRIS)

From the day he was born, Nicholas Brendon boasted a gift that most people don't have: an identical twin brother, Kelly. Born April 12, 1971, the pair were inseparable, and to this day remain best friends. "You always had a person to play with," says Nick of Kelly. "You always had someone

Nicholas Brendon signs his autograph for a fan.
SAMIEL

to confide in, someone to talk to. And someone just to beat up" ("Q&A with Nicholas Brendon"). His parents got divorced when he was young, and it brought him and his brothers (he also has two younger ones) even closer together.

As a child, Nick developed a stutter, and had a terrible time with it, especially in high school. One of the reasons he was attracted to the script of *Buffy the Vampire Slayer* was because of his own rotten time at high school. "High school isn't really great to many people," he says. "It's like a mandatory prison sentence. . . . In Israel they make you join the army, in America we go to high school" (qtd. in Owen). To add to his stutter, he had an acne problem (one thing that no one seems to suffer from on *Buffy*) that made him so upset he refused to go out anymore. But he remembers his mother's optimistic attitude at the time. "My mom would say, 'Nick, love the zits. Love them. Embrace them.

Because it means that you have oily skin, and as you get older, you won't have any wrinkles.' Now I'm 27 and I'm playing 17. So it's like, God bless you, Mom" ("Q&A with Nicholas Brendon").

After high school he worked as a receptionist at a talent agency and as a waiter, and was a pre-med student, but he knew he had to conquer his stuttering. So he decided to go into the one career that would find a stutter unacceptable: acting. It took him over four years to overcome it, saying tongue twisters and speaking more slowly, but when he finally stopped stuttering, it was the most rewarding accomplishment of his life.

He moved to Los Angeles, but had a terrible time trying to find parts. He started getting bit roles in television shows and movies, but he couldn't win any bigger parts. Although his résumé said something much different. "My whole resume is pretty much a lie," he said. "I did one day on *Young and the Restless* and then, of course, I put on my résumé 'recurring' because it looks better. And now I've gone from that to being a regular. So it's out of control" (qtd. in Pierce, "Role"). He hit rock bottom a few months before landing the role of Xander on *Buffy the Vampire Slayer* when, as a waiter, he could barely pay his rent, his girlfriend had left him, and he had all but given up hope of ever finding a good acting role. He was then hired on as a production assistant on *Dave's World*, but he says now the position was more of a gopher job than anything else. "I had to go and buy Pop Tarts for the writers, and they wanted the cinnamon Pop Tarts, but not the ones with the frosting on top, so if I got the frosting on top I was in a world of hurt" (*Vibe*). When he didn't show a lot of enthusiasm in the workplace, he was ultimately brought into his boss's office and fired, with these last words: "You should be acting" (qtd. in Rudolph). Three months later, he won the role of Xander, essentially his first big acting role.

Today he lives in a brand-new home high above Los Angeles, where he can look down on the city lights at night. "It's like the Peter Pan ride at Disneyland," he laughs (qtd. in Rudolph). The only downside of his fame is the effect it has had on his brother, who often gets mistaken for him and has to dodge autograph hounds. Kelly has had to dye his hair blond to try to avoid the mistaken identity. "And I can see how that can be a bit cumbersome," says Nick, "because I love him very much" ("Q&A with Nicholas Brendon").

Considering Nick only started acting when he was 20 and is now on one of the hottest shows on television, it's probably safe to say he has a long career ahead of him. And he knows that acting is his calling in life. "I would like to entertain people," he says. "I love to do that. Thank you, God" ("Q&A with Nicholas Brendon").

SETH GREEN
(OZ)

Seth Green has been in more movies than anyone else on *Buffy the Vampire Slayer*. He was the guy who popularized the phrase "Cha-ching!" and he was the last member of the *Buffy* cast to be signed on as a regular. Seth has had a long and illustrious career, and he's only 24 years old.

Born on February 8, 1974, Seth grew up in Philadelphia with his math-teacher father, Herb, his artist mother, Barbara, and his sister, Kaela. He made his acting debut at the age of six in a production of *Hello, Dolly!* and decided he wanted to be an actor right then and there. He has never wavered from that decision. Realizing her son was serious, Barbara made sure he got an education — he did correspondence courses and was tutored on the set — and he

Seth Green
ERIKA ROTTLER

had plenty of opportunities as an actor. He has tried acting classes, but attributes most of his acting knowledge to what he learned on the job. His first movie was *The Hotel New Hampshire*, with Rob Lowe and Jodie Foster, and that small part led to a large role in Woody Allen's *Radio Days*. Seth enjoyed working with Allen, and appreciated the fact that the director didn't expect him to be a little adult: "There was one point where we were running around with water-guns and stuff, and he allowed that to happen" (qtd. in Green, "Werewolf").

His next film was *My Stepmother Is an Alien*, where he met and worked with Alyson Hannigan for the first time. They became very close friends, keeping in touch after the movie was finished. "We had a funny relationship," he says. "We would not see each other for a year, and then we'd get in touch and hang out really intensely for about three weeks, and then that would sort of peter off" (qtd. in Green, "Werewolf"). Following that film he appeared in several others, including *Big Business*, *Pump Up the Volume*, *White Man's Burden*, *To Gillian on Her 37th Birthday*, and *Austin Powers: International Man of Mystery*. In the latter film, Seth played Scott Evil, the son of Dr. Evil, played by Mike Myers. Seth enjoyed working on the movie, but said Myers was so funny it was difficult to keep from laughing all the time. "You can see me break in the movie at one point," he says. "He'd just done the 'Macarena,' then he walks to me, you see me turn and almost smile, and then I got it together" ("Live Star Chat with Seth Green").

Despite enjoying the various movies he worked on, Seth also guest-starred in many of the hottest shows on tele-vision, including *Mad About You*, *The Wonder Years*, *Weird Science*, *The Drew Carey Show*, *Cybill*, and the pilot episode of *The X-Files*. However, it was actually a part in a strange commercial that made him a recognizable face. In 1997 he appeared in a Rally's commercial as a drive-through cashier annoying the customers — he and another atten-dant would pretend they were ringing in the orders by yelling "Cha-ching!" after every customer order. That silly line became a popular catch phrase. He says he still gets recognized as that guy in the Rally's commercial, and was stunned to find out how popular it had become. "It got out of hand. It was so silly. That's what happens with a catch phrase — people get caught up" ("Live Star Chat").

That same year he showed up for an audition with Joss Whedon, who recognized him from *My Stepmother Is an Alien*. "I had these big, crappy glasses on," he remembers. "I read with Joss and he asked me to take my glasses off" ("Live Star Chat"). Unlike the others, Seth had to audition only once before he was given the role. He called Alyson that night to let her know they'd be working together again. No one was certain that his would be a recurring role, and when he was offered the opportunity to become a regular cast member, he hesitated at first, but decided to take the part. "I weighed my options as to what else I could be doing, and decided that this was the best show I could be on right now, the best character I could be playing, the best potential" (qtd. in Green, "Werewolf"). And despite all the other experience he has had, he enjoys television more than movies because of the challenges it presents.

Seth loves Oz's character, who he says is based on someone Joss knew while he was at college. "The thing I love about Oz is that he doesn't say anything unless it's important, so when he has something to say, it's really thought out. Smart" (qtd. in Green, "Werewolf"). The biggest challenge on the show so far has been when Oz turned into a werewolf. Although Seth was happy with how the episode turned out, he says the makeup people, headed by Emmy-award-winning makeup artist Todd McIntosh, had only two weeks to prepare the costume. Seth had to sit for hours for all the hair to be applied, and then the sequence lasted a matter of seconds.

So now that he's a regular on *Buffy*, will he be settling down and focusing his energies on the show? Not a chance. He has four movies in the works, and starred in the summer film *Can't Hardly Wait* with Jennifer Love Hewitt.

His other films include *Enemy of the State* (late 1998), starring Will Smith, Jon Voigt, Ian Hart, Jamie Kennedy, Jason Lee, and Jason Robards, where he plays a member of the National Security team that is chasing Will Smith. He's very excited about a 1999 release, *Stonebrook*, which he says is a cross between *The Sting* and *The Usual Suspects*. He'll also be starring in an independent film, *The Attic Expeditions*, and *Idle Hands*. Seth has completed more films in his 24 years than most actors do in a lifetime. And he doesn't intend to stop now.

* * *

If you would like to contact any of the cast members of the show, including Sarah Michelle Gellar, send fan mail to them care of:

> Buffy the Vampire Slayer
> The Warner Brothers Television Network
> 4000 Warner Blvd.
> Burbank, CA 91522

Because of their busy schedules, not all of the actors might be able to reply to you, but to improve your chances, include a self-addressed, stamped envelope.

BUFFY THE VAMPIRE SLAYER WEB SITES

It would be impossible to list all the *Buffy the Vampire Slayer* Web sites — there are literally hundreds of them. This is a short list to get you started if you're new to the game. Most of the sites belong to Web rings, which is where you join a circle of like-minded sites and put an icon at the bottom of your opening page. When someone visits the site, they can move to the next site in the ring by clicking on the "Next" button. It's a fast and easy way to see many different sites, one after the other. I have included a few sites devoted to specific cast members, but the list here is limited to my personal favorites. There are sites devoted to just about every character you can think of on the show, so don't despair if your favorite isn't listed here. It's bound to be out there somewhere. . . .

Buffy the Vampire Slayer Official Site
www.buffy.com
One thing that seems to be constant among Web sites devoted to television shows is that the official sites are never as good as the fans' sites. Well, this one is the exception. This is an amazing site with a haunting, gothic look to it, and it's possibly the single most popular *Buffy the Vampire Slayer* site on the Internet. The posting board, known as The Bronze, is one of the most popular sections of this site, where fans can post messages to each other and to stars of the show. Seth Green, David Boreanaz, Joss Whedon, Jeff Pruitt (stunt coordinator),

Address: http://www.great.buffy.info

and Alyson Hannigan are some of the more frequent VIP's on the board and in the chat rooms. (You'll know them because their names come up in vibrant colors when they post.) Other sections include bios of the show's main stars, a detailed plot summary for each of the past episodes, an online interactive game where you battle Moloch (who is inside your computer), a spot to join the official *Buffy the Vampire Slayer* fan club, and much more.

Sonja Marie's Buffy the Vampire Slayer Links
www.planetx.com/~sonja/btvsurls/btvsurls.html
If you're planning to sit down and surf the best *Buffy* sites, forget every other search engine — this comprehensive list of *Buffy* links will lead you to wherever you want to roam. A massive achievement, and deserving of all the praise it receives.

The Slayer's FanFic Archive
www.slayerfanfic.com/
This is the biggest archive of *Buffy* fan fiction (stories written by fans based on the characters and events in the show), with series of stories, short stories, poems, unfinished works, and much more. The quality of the stories ranges from okay to "This should be a script!" There are indexes of authors and stories to help ease your search, and transcripts of every episode of *Buffy the Vampire Slayer*, which in itself is a monumental achievement. In addition there is a section for readers to post their comments, as well as a page of tips — grammar, sentence structure, creative aids — to help any budding writer. A terrific site!

Domain of the Slain
www2.uic.edu/~ahufan1/btvs/
Domain of the Slain is a *must* for all *Buffy* fans. Willow is your guide, and the most interesting aspect of this site

is the "Written, Not Scene" section, where you get to see the scenes that were in the script but were cut out of the final version of the episodes. Check out what you missed! There are also rare and behind-the-scenes pictures that are really fascinating, a list of songs, and quotations from each episode (and some of the *Buffy* books), the best schedule of upcoming appearances and events, and a great list of links. An awesome site.

Buffy Music Site
**www.geocities.com/Hollywood/Lot/8864/
music.htm**
One of the most effective elements on *Buffy the Vampire Slayer* is the use of music to illustrate each scene. If you've ever fallen in love with a particular song, or seen a band that appealed to you onstage at The Bronze, check out this page to find out what the song title is and where you can buy it, learn about the band, find out if they're on tour and where, and read the lyrics to the songs. This is an *amazing* site, and hands-down one of my top-five favorites.

BtVS: Slayer Central
members.tripod.com/~slayercentral/
This is a great site that has all the latest news on the actors, books, episodes, a guide to what episode will be airing each week and when, information on how to mail the actors, fan fiction, a Web-site rating page, and much more.

Address: http://www.great.buffy.info

Sunnydale High School's Home Page
www.sunnydale.simplenet.com
This is one of the most clever *Buffy* pages around. It's set
up to look like an actual high school home page, complete with administrative information (which gives you
ways to contact the Web site administrator), a message
from the principal's office (where he mentions they are
in need of a new swim coach, computer science teacher,
and school nurse), a map of the school (based on watching where people go during episodes — it's quite fascinating), tests and examinations (where you must answer
questions pertaining to each episode), and much, much
more. The latest news on the show pops up on the opening page, and there is info about the stars and the crew
members. Brilliant concept, and well executed.

The Sounds of the Slayer
techzero.simplenet.com/buffy/
If it's Buffy sound files you're looking for, this is the place
to find them. You can download all the best one-liners
from this site, and program them into your computer for
special occasions. Might I suggest as the start-up sound
for your computer: "Hi, for those of you who have just
tuned in, everyone here is a crazy person."

Giles' Stacks
www.znet.com/~volterra/giles/giles.html
This is a fascinating site hosted by "Giles" himself, where
you get to look through his books. In actuality the site
sends you to different links that pertain to individual

episodes. For example, for "Phases" it sends you to Web sites about werewolves. A wonderful site, and one I wish I'd found much earlier!

Sunnydale School Library
www.geocities.com/Area51/Cavern/1763/ buffy.html
This is an interesting little place where you can "browse the shelves" of the library, which consist of lists of reading material pertaining to the show, including books about vampires, werewolves, and monsters, and any other re-search that slayerettes might like to undertake in their spare time. It also includes lists of favorite quotations from each episode, the *Buffy* Drinking Game, and a link to join the *Buffy the Vampire Slayer* mailing list.

Hades' Underworld
www.geocities.com/Area51/Chamber/5851/
This very good-looking site is worth checking out just to see its banners. It's updated to incorporate the latest episodes, has lots of photos, a quiz, an episode guide, and more.

Sites Devoted to Cast Members

The Sarah Michelle Gellar Fan Page
smgfan.com
The Sarah Michelle Gellar fan page. Photos, biography, articles about all aspects of her career — you name it, it's here. The page is maintained by Lawless, who has done a fabulous job culling old photos, information, and articles all about Sarah. There is even a link to the very

popular game Six Degrees of Separation, where you type in Sarah's name and the name of another celebrity to see if they can link her to the other person in six steps or less. Try and stump them. I tried every obscure actor's name I could think of and couldn't do it. This is the numero uno Sarah page: if you're looking for anything about her, begin your search here.

Sarah Michelle Gellar: Brighter than Any Star in the Sky
www.sarah-michelle-gellar.com/
This site stands out not only for everything it has to offer, but because the Web site administrator updates it every few days, keeping everyone up-to-date on the latest information about Sarah Michelle Gellar and *Buffy the Vampire Slayer*. There is a calendar where you can see at a glance when Sarah will be making any television appearances, and there are articles, photos, sound clips, a tape trade ring, favorite Sarah quotes, a link to the Sarah Michelle Gellar mailing list, a chat room (which comes to life Mondays and Fridays at 7 PM), movie clips, and much more. This page is second only to the Sarah Michelle Gellar Fan Page.

Alyson Hannigan Appreciation Society
www.network23.com/hub/ahas/
After Sarah Michelle Gellar pages, the ones devoted to Willow and Alyson Hannigan are the best. This site features exclusive photos, the latest news on Alyson, chat transcripts, "Willowisms" (favorite Willow quotes), a brief bio, stats, and much more. Very well done.

The Alyson Hannigan Altar
users.twave.net/shrine/ahaltar.htm
This is a page that lives up to its name. Alyson once mentioned she was upgrading her computer to Windows 98, so the sweet thing about this site is that the Web site

administrator anticipates she'll drop by for a visit, and has added little notes to her throughout. Very up-to-date, with lots of information about Alyson and tons of links to other sites. This is a must-see.

The Babe Known as Xander
xander.interspeed.net/
I love this site! If you're looking for Nicholas Brendon info, look no further than this one, if only for the great animated logo at the beginning that reads, "For Each Generation, There is Only One Xander." Biography, filmography, pictures, articles, Xanderisms, links — you name it, this fun site has got it. A must-see for Xander fans.

Phoenix's David Boreanaz Cool Stuff
www.david-boreanaz.com/
This is the best Boreanaz site, featuring pictures, links, all of David's online chats and articles, and many of his comments from when he went onto the Buffy posting board on the official site.

The Official Seth Green Homepage
www.geocities.com/Hollywood/Set/1503/
If you're a fan of the man they call Oz, this is the place for you. Seth authorized this page as his official one after chatting with the fans who made it, and it's a terrific tribute to this fine actor. You'll get updated information on his latest movies and other acting pursuits, lots of rare photos, a biography and filmography, and other goodies.

Address: http://www.great.buffy.info

Keepers

If you belong to any of the mailing lists, you'll notice a strange phenomenon in many of the signature lines in the posts: the members of the list "keep" things belonging to cast members. If you see something in an episode that appeals to you, like Willow's little green frog, you can go to the Willow keeper site and apply to become the keeper of that object (and, for your information, the frog has been taken). As the keeper, you promise to protect it, and although you can't actually do that, it's a great way to become part of the show itself. You can also become a guardian, which is where you protect something intangible, like Cordelia's condescending attitude toward Willow (sorry, that's taken, too). It's a lot of fun.

Here are the sites for the main characters, but if you are interested in keeping something related to a secondary character or someone not listed here, try the Master Index (first site listed) and you'll probably find a link to it.

Master Index to Buffy Keeper Sites
www.concentric.net/~Creatv/keeper/index.html

Giles Keepers
**www.geocities.com/TelevisionCity/7728/
gaspers.html**
E-mail the president of the fan club at gaspers@eskimo. com and she'll provide you with a list of the items that are already taken.

Cordelia Keepers
members.aol.com/PalOBuffys/Keepers.html

Oz Keepers
**www.geocities.com/TelevisionCity/9102/
ozGA.html**

Willow Keepers
www.concentric.com/~creatv/willow/index.html

Buffy Keepers
www.geocities.com/Hollywood/Academy/6358/
(This one is huge — look out!)

Jenny Calendar Keepers
www.angelfire.com/ca/MCTP/mctp.html

Xander Keepers
www.geocities.com/~xanderkeepers

The Weird and the Quirky

The Buffy/Bond Crossover Page
www.mindspring.com/~big.al/buffybond/
Featuring the ongoing story *Goldenfang*, this hilarious page mixes the conventions of James Bond movies with the dialogue of *Buffy*. Definitely worth checking out.

Address: http://www.great.buffy.info

Sunnydale Cemetery
www.geocities.com/Hollywood/Theater/3799/
Morbid much? I had to include this site because it's one of the strangest ones I found. There are graves, urns, and monuments for every character who has died on the show, including many vampires. There is even a section where you can reserve and design graves for those who haven't yet died. This site is extremely ghoulish and creepy — which is probably why I loved it so much.

Nielsen Ratings for Buffy the Vampire Slayer
www.iaw.on.ca/~rohaly/tvschedule/buffy.html
This site meticulously keeps track of the ratings for each episode, listing how many people watched when the episodes first aired and all the reruns. Check how your favorite episode ranks against the others.

Wallflowers Home Page
www.geocities.com/Wellesley/4149/
Okay, okay, I realize I've got more Alyson Hannigan pages here than anything else, but I just had to include this one for having the best name of all the *Buffy* pages. Wallflowers stands for **W**ondrous **A**lyson's **L**ifelong **L**obby **F**or **L**audation **O**f **W**illow's **E**ggheadedness, **R**efinement & **S**exiness. That was just too brilliant to pass up.

COULD YOU BE A SLAYER? THE BUFFY THE VAMPIRE SLAYER TRIVIA QUIZ

So, you think you know everything there is to know about *Buffy the Vampire Slayer*? Well, here's the place to test your skills. You'll be asked questions about specific episodes, quotations, and characters. But be warned: Some of these questions are very difficult. The answers begin on page 189, but I suggest that you answer each question on a piece of paper, rather than looking back and forth between the questions and the answers; otherwise you might accidentally see the answers to future questions. Good luck!

XANDERISMS

Since the first episode, Xander has consistently had some of the funniest one-liners on the show. See if you can name the episode where he says the following lines.

1. "You're not gonna yak on me, are you?"
2. "The quality of mercy is not Buffy."

3. "I wish dating was like slaying: You know, simple, direct, stake to the heart, no muss, no fuss."

4. "I laugh in the face of danger! Then I hide until it goes away."

5. "I'm 17. Looking at linoleum makes me wanna have sex."

6. "We're your bosom friends! The friends of your bosom!"

7. "All right, but if you come across the army of zombies, can you page us before they eat your flesh?"

8. "Looks like Mr. Caution Man, but the sound he makes is funny."

9. "I knew you were lying. . . . Undead Liar Guy."

10. " 'Something weird is going on.' Isn't that our school motto?"

WHAT'S MY LINE?

For this section you must answer **who said the line** and **in which episode**.

1. "You were right, all along, about everything — well, no, you weren't right about your mother coming back as a Pekinese."

2. "I seem to be having a slight case of nudity here."

3. "Oh, right, 'cause I lie awake at night hoping you tweakos will be my best friends. And that my first husband will be a balding, demented, homeless man."

4. "I've known you for two minutes and I can't stand you. I don't really feature you living forever."

5. "God! I am so mentally challenged!"

6. "I had very definite plans about my future. I was going to be a fighter pilot. Or possibly a grocer."

7. "We all need help with our feelings. Otherwise we bottle them up, and before you know it, powerful laxatives are involved."

8. "If I say something you really don't want to hear, do you promise not to bite me?"

9. "See, in my fantasy, when I'm kissing you, you're kissing me."

10. "Don't worry, roller-boy. I've got everything under control."

11. "Thanks for the wake-up, but I'll stick with my clock radio."

12. "There are things I will not tolerate: students loitering on campus after school, horrible murders with hearts being removed. And also smoking."

13. "Don't tell me people still fall for that Anne Rice routine."

14. "It's safe to say that in his animal state, his idea of wooing doesn't involve a Yanni CD and a bottle of Chianti."

15. "Who died and made you Elvis?"

16. "I don't stand for this kind of malarkey in my house!"

17. "If you're gonna crack jokes, then I'm gonna pull out your ribcage and wear it as a hat."

18. "She's evil, okay, way eviler than me!"

19. "What's with the Catholic schoolgirl look? Last time I saw you, it was kimonos."

20. "I'll crack him like an egg!"

WHO'S WHO?

You've identified their quotations, now see how well you know the characters.

1. How does Xander find out that Buffy is the slayer?

2. How did Colin become the Anointed One?

3. What is the name of Willow's father? (Give yourself one bonus point if you can name the episode in which we find out.)

4. Drusilla was almost killed in this European city.

5. How old is Spike?

6. What two characters on the show were dying of brain cancer?

7. Which character is a fan of the Bay City Rollers?

8. What is Oz's ambition in life?

9. This character kept wanting to play Parcheesi.

10. Name the nerdy guy who gets picked on in several episodes and eventually gets interrogated by Willow.

11. What exactly is Whistler?

12. What ultimately happened to Amy's mother?

13. This character is the first student Buffy talks to at Sunnydale High.

14. Which vampire was the Master's favorite?

15. Angel turned Drusilla into a vampire right after she had done this.

EPISODE EVENTS

Match up the episode with its events.

1. Name the two episodes where Oz's band plays at The Bronze.

2. What was the name of the fraternity in "Reptile Boy"?

3. In "Prophecy Girl," what does Xander go home and do to take away the pain of Buffy's rejection?

4. What strange event is happening at The Bronze in "Angel"?

5. What did Angel write on the wall after killing Jenny's Uncle Enyos?

6. In what two episodes are students looking at the cheer-leading trophy?

7. Name the two episodes in which a police chief questions Joyce about Buffy.

8. When Angel loses his soul, who is the first person he kills?

9. In what episode do Willow and Cordelia discuss guy problems while at The Bronze?

10. In "Inca Mummy Girl," what does Xander teach Ampata to do while they are sitting in the bleachers?

11. Name the two episodes in which Xander and Cordelia end up in Buffy's basement.

12. In "School Hard," Buffy chops vegetables with this strange utensil.

13. Name the episode in which Buffy clears the school fence with a single backward leap.

14. In what episode does Willow invite Angel into her room?

15. Name the two episodes in which Oz is shot.

16. In which episode does Xander daydream about being a guitarist in a rock band?

17. Buffy has punched Giles twice on the show. In which episodes?

18. In "Go Fish," Willow compares being eviscerated to this.

19. In what episode does the cafeteria food turn into snakes?

20. Name the two episodes in which we see Cordy's license plate.

21. In which two episodes does Oz see Willow and ask himself, "Who is that girl?"

22. In "Halloween," a vampire videotapes Buffy doing this.

THERE'S A FIRST TIME FOR EVERYTHING

Name the episode in which each of these events occurs on the show for the first time.

1. Giles finds one of Xander's jokes funny.
2. Cordelia and Xander exchange insults.
3. Giles and Jenny go out on a date.
4. Cordelia saves someone's life.
5. We hear that Buffy keeps a diary.
6. Buffy tells Willow about her parents' divorce.
7. We actually see a student take out a book from the library.
8. Oz sees a vampire get staked.
9. We see Buffy at the mall.
10. Giles realizes Angel doesn't cast a reflection in the glass.
11. We see Xander's room.
12. Buffy escapes from her room through the window.
13. We see Giles' ancient car.
14. Oz and Willow speak to each other.
15. Giles and Joyce meet.

TRUE OR FALSE?

Answer the following questions "true" or "false" and correct the false statements.

1. Giles graduated from Oxford University in England.
2. When Buffy finds out that Owen reads Emily Dickinson, she gushes that he's "sensitive, yet manly."
3. Angel says he came to America about 80 years ago.

4. When Giles finds out about the tattoo that Ethan gave Buffy, he offers to help pay for its removal.

5. Willow says her greatest disappointment is that she never learned to play a musical instrument.

6. Xander pretended not to remember what happened in "The Pack" because he was disgusted that he'd eaten Principal Flutie.

7. Xander's aptitude test says he would make a good prison guard.

8. Cordelia's younger sister is very intelligent and refuses to be a cheerleader.

9. Buffy thinks the May Queen tradition is ridiculous.

10. Oz's uncle is a werewolf.

T
R
I
V
I
A

Q
U
I
Z

A NIGHT
TO REMEMBER:
THE BUFFY POSTING
BOARD PARTY
FEBRUARY 14, 1998

This chapter was written with the help of the following posting board members who attended the party: Erika Rottler (a.k.a. Sasheer), Erika Gilbert (a.k.a. Batra), Keith Miller (a.k.a. KAM), Tammie Purcell (a.k.a. greengirl), Viet My Nguyen (a.k.a. Samiel), Karri Phillips (a.k.a. Phoenix), and Will York (a.k.a. fenric).

It was the kind of thing fans dream of, and the kind of thing celebrities tend not to do. Imagine this: You're in an Internet chat room one night talking with other people who share a love for a certain television show. You get to know everyone really well, and one day someone comes up with the idea that you should all get together at one big party. Then someone else says he knows the people on the show, and he might be able to get them to come. You fly in to California for a night of meeting your fellow posting-board members, only to be met with almost the entire cast of the show.

This is exactly what happened to almost 100 *Buffy the Vampire Slayer* fans on February 14, 1998.

Every day the fans would meet on the posting board, known as The Bronze, and discuss the show, the characters, or just chat about life in general. If you were lucky, you'd be in The Bronze when one of the "VIPs" would come in. The VIPs include David Boreanaz, Seth Green, Nicholas Brendon, Alyson Hannigan, and Joss Whedon, and the VIPs who post on the board regularly are Jeff Pruitt (stunt coordinator), Ty King (writer), and RD (the assistant to David Greenwalt, the show's co-executive producer). The fans were from all over North America, and since very few of them had met before, one of the posters, known as Blade, came up with the idea that they should get together and meet. Another poster, AKA Becker, immediately agreed, and said it could be held in LA because that's where the show is filmed. Todd McIntosh (the show's makeup artist) started spreading the word around the set, seeing if anyone was interested. Eventually RD stepped in to help out. The ball was now rolling.

Alyson was the first of the cast members who agreed to attend the party, and a committee of posters was formed to work out the details and coordinate who was coming. Although they knew about the VIPs who would be attending, they decided to keep the information under wraps, because they didn't want people to come solely for the purpose of meeting cast members. The purpose of the party was to meet fellow Bronzers — the VIPs were a bonus. RD came through and said that he got most of the cast to agree to come, and he also booked the spot for the event. Those posters who said they'd be there for sure and sent in their money (to cover costs of renting the place) were given an invitation with the location of the event — Planet Hollywood in Los Angeles — which was kept secret from the other posters. However, the PBP (Posting Board

Party) Committee were surprised to learn that the day before the event, Planet Hollywood publicly announced that cast members from *Buffy the Vampire Slayer* would be appearing there, and so fans from all over California would show up to see them.

On February 13, posters flew in from Texas, New York, Florida, Canada, Washington DC, New Jersey, Illinois, Indiana, North Carolina, Washington, Georgia, and Wisconsin — one of the committee members estimates that 90 percent of the attendees were from out of town. (Is that true fandom or what?) AKA Becker lost all of his luggage upon arrival in Los Angeles, but he put his chin up and simply bought more clothes. Another member, Samiel, laughed when he remembered the problems that occurred when posters tried to meet up with people they'd never seen. Considering most of the posters go by amusing aliases, Samiel explains, "One does not go up to a stranger in an airport and ask questions such as, 'Are you Dead Boy?' I guess that is one of the many disadvantages of knowing someone only by their Internet nickname." To make things easier, however, at the PBP everyone was given a name tag with their Internet handle.

The party was to start at six, but the committee arrived early to set up. RD was there helping out the committee members, who worked out security and figured out where people would go. Initially Planet Hollywood said the party could be held up on the second floor, but then switched it to the first floor so it would be more readily accessible to the posting-board members. However, the committee had to rope off a special section for the party to keep out people who hadn't been invited. Planet Hollywood provided them with finger foods, pasta, and free non-alcoholic beverages, and the committee had arranged for a huge chocolate cake designed to look like the posting board. The members of the posting board mingled about, excited beyond words about the cast members who were about to arrive, but when the *Buffy the Vampire Slayer* theme song began to play over the Planet Hollywood sound system, everyone broke out into a cheer and turned the evening into a real party.

David Boreanaz was the first cast member to arrive (other VIPs had arrived earlier), and it was then that people realized what a madhouse the evening would turn out to be. Some of the posters mobbed him, wanting autographs, pictures, and just to shake his hand. As poster Batra put it, "It was as if David were a long-lost Beatle, the awed look on their faces, and one of the girls looked like she was about to cry." RD darted through the crowd to rescue David and lead him upstairs where he could have his dinner before joining the party. Because he was the first to arrive, he probably garnered the most excitement. Erika Rottler remembers, "Seeing him for the first time was the only time I felt starstruck. There was Angel."

Soon after David's grand entrance, other members of the cast and crew arrived one by one — Anthony Stewart Head, Nicholas Brendon, Ty King, Jeff Pruitt, Sophia Crawford (Sarah's stunt double), Joss Whedon, Todd McIntosh, Marti Noxon (writer/story editor), Alyson Hannigan, and Seth Green. Also in attendance was James Lamb, known as TV James, who had created the first official *Buffy the Vampire Slayer* Web site that had brought all of the people together. (His design was adopted for the look of the new posting board as well.)

The posting-board members who contributed to this chapter had stories about every VIP who was there. Everyone said that Jeff and Sophia, who had initially met while working on *The Mighty Morphin Power Rangers*, made a very attractive couple. The two had gotten engaged a few weeks before the party, during the filming of "Phases." A regular on the posting board, Jeff often indulges the fans by talking about filming the episodes and has even scanned in story-boards to show people. Erika, who has kept in touch with Jeff and Sophia since the party, had only nice things to say about Jeff: "Jeff is one of the coolest people around. If it wasn't for him I would have no idea about stunt people behind the scenes. He made me see a whole new side of Hollywood." The PBP wasn't the first time Erika had met Sophia Crawford, but she is always surprised at what Sophia looks like in person: "You would expect a big, tough, scary woman, but when you shake her hand and look into her eyes you see the true beauty in her. She is one of the sweetest people I have ever met."

David Boreanaz got rave reviews from everyone, and people kept commenting on how nice he was. Karri Phillips recalls a group of girls who were about 13 years old who had been eating at the restaurant and recognized David when he arrived. They dashed down the street to buy copies of a teen magazine whose cover David graced and returned in the hopes that he might sign them. Because they weren't part of the PBP, they had to stand aside and look on, until David finally spotted them standing behind the ropes. He walked over, signed all the magazines, and then chatted with them, proving to everyone how gracious he was. Later, the father of a young boy approached one of the party members and asked if it would be possible to get David to sign an autograph for his son. David obliged, and found the little guy hiding behind a pillar out of shyness. Noticing the boy's Chicago Bulls jacket, David talked to him about the Bulls game the night before and put the boy at ease.

One posting board member couldn't make the party because she was studying for her bar exam, but the other Bronzers knew what a big fan she was of David. One of the posters had been talking to her from his cell phone, keeping her updated on the evening's events, and he handed the phone to David so she could talk to him. Everyone was pleased to discover how genuine David was, and Keith Miller says that over the course of the evening David posed for numerous photos and talked to everyone there. Tammie Purcell and Will York talked to David at one point, saying they preferred him as the evil Angelus. He was very open and animated with them, explaining how he prepared for the change in his behavior, but he wouldn't give away any of the upcoming episodes. Tammie joked that Angel needed to kill someone who was close to Buffy, but who wouldn't really shake up the story line, like Buffy's father. David laughed out loud at the idea and said he thought it was very funny, but added, "Just wait." David was slyly referring to "Passion," which had not yet aired.

Karri also talked to David at length, and recalls one trick he played on her. "At one point during the party, he walked up to me and said, 'Would you like a kiss?' and of course I look at him with a blank stare. Then he hands me a little Hershey's Kiss." She laughs that she ended up getting four real kisses out of him later in the evening, when her friend was trying to take a picture of David kissing her and the camera (luckily) wouldn't work.

Joss Whedon might not have an instantly recognizable face for most fans, but because he is the true mastermind behind the show he is treated with awe and respect among the fans and the cast and crew. Many fans got their pictures taken with him, but one Bronzer in particular, known as -mere-, was well-known as a big fan of Joss. Samiel recalls that when Joss first arrived, people started chanting for her to come over. "The chant was '-mere-' first softly, and finally so loud nothing else could be heard. . . . Joss and -mere- met in an embrace and the applause shook the room like thunder."

Batra was shocked when Joss immediately recognized her name from the posting board. Will York said he got to talk to Joss at length, and remembers, "He talked of how he *wasn't* working on several projects that had been rumored (*Planet of the Apes*, *Avatar*, *Dr. Who*, etc.), because he was devoting his focus to *Buffy*. I also presented him with a membership card in Sarah-SOTA (the Sarah Society of True Adoration, a club I founded on the board), which he dug. . . ." Joss had brought along some behind-the-scenes and bloopers tapes, made especially for this event, which were playing on the monitors throughout the evening.

Nicholas Brendon was very entertaining, and people mentioned him especially in conjunction with the Xander Dance Club (XDC). At the beginning of "Angel," Xander is at The Bronze doing a crazy dance, trying to get other girls to dance with him. Two of the posting-board members — KAM and Little Willow — thought that scene was so funny they formed the online XDC. The club essentially began as a joke, but others joined in and it soon became the biggest club on the posting board (later to be surpassed by Little Willow's We Possess Willow Power club). To join the XDC you simply had to give a valid reason you wanted to be in, and you were assigned a number. Many members chose mottos as well, and they discuss the songs in the show and create scenarios where Xander must dance.

At the Posting Board Party, the XDC had bought a plaque for Nick. At the LA comic convention, an XDC member, Glitergrrl, had told Nick about the club, and he accepted an honorary membership as Member #0. So Keith had had the names of the members of the club engraved on the plaque with Nick's status as Member #0 placed at the top. They presented it to Nick in front of everyone at the party, but some of the women in the audience shouted out that he should earn his plaque by pulling off some Xander moves right there. Joss and Jeff started to coax him — Joss joked that he'd give him a raise — and Nick finally agreed.

But he had one condition. Grabbing the microphone, he said he would dance only if David danced, too. Karri had been talking to David and his friend Patrick when this happened, and she said he kind of sighed to himself and relented. Patrick was floored, saying to Karri, "I can't believe David is dancing. He *doesn't* dance!"

As David walked toward the floor, Nick continued to joke around at the microphone. "Most of you guys know David as Brooding Guy," he said. "But I know David. He isn't really Brooding Guy, he's Happy Dance Guy. And why is that, David?" "Because of the '*fun*'!" David laughed. They both performed a series of hilarious dance moves, with "Nick pulling an Elvis and David pulling a . . . I'm not quite sure what he was doing out there," laughs Erika. Keith remembers the scene clearly: "Amid screams and cheering, the two of them whipped around the dance floor in the fun and uniquely Xanderesque style. Nick, in a very Elvis-like routine, spun his arms, tap-danced, and even pulled off the splits, finally ending in an exhausted bow." After the two had finished, Nick graciously accepted his award, joking, "Number zero — is that a good thing?" For many, the dance was the highlight of the evening.

Nick was a hit among fans on a personal level as well. Erika says, "Nick had that dark, charming quality with a dazzling smile to go along with it. He was very open to compliments and seemed to truly be enjoying the work he is doing on the show." "Bewitched, Bothered and Bewildered" had aired a few days earlier, and Erika congratulated him on what many fans consider one of the best episodes of the season. He was very touched and obviously loves working with Charisma. When Erika told him how happy she was that the two had become a couple on the show, he answered, "Isn't that great?" Tammie Purcell joked that momentarily she became Nick's drink holder when he was asked for an autograph. She laughs, "Was I

Above: David Boreanaz, who was the first to arrive
at the party, receives a smooch from Seth Green . . .
Below: . . . and gives one back to Alyson Hannigan.

Above: Sophia Crawford, who is Sarah Michelle Gellar's stunt double, and her fiancé Jeff Pruitt, the show's stunt coordinator.
Below: Joss Whedon, the master of all things *Buffy*, arrives at the party.

Above: Anthony Stewart Head talks to a fan.

Below: Nicholas Brendon (right) talks Boreanaz into dancing with him.

KARRI PHILLIPS

Above: David dances to the delight of the audience,
while Nick watches from the sidelines.
Below: Can you contort your body like this?

KEITH MILLER

Above: Alyson Hannigan and Seth Green,
close friends in real life as well as on screen.
Below: Jeff and Sophia laugh hysterically as Nick
and David show off their synchronized dancing.

Above: What would you give to be the fan in the middle?

Below: David wants to chat with fans online.

Above: Nick, who charmed everyone at the party, poses with a fan.

Below: David puts the squeeze on Alyson.

Above: Tony, Nick, David, and Seth
play vampires to Alyson's willing victim.
Below: The gang says hello to the posting board
members who couldn't make it to the party.

HI EVERYBODY
I MISS YOU!!!

POSTING BOARD
RULES!!!

tempted to take the straw? Yes I was. . . . but I showed restraint."

Nick wasn't the only VIP to receive gifts. One of the committee members came up with a very clever idea that whoever came from out of town should bring a postcard from their hometown, and all the postcards were presented to Joss. Alyson Hannigan was given a glass dolphin, beanie babies, and a toy clapping monkey (because of the dream sequence in "Surprise"). Tony was given a scone mix and English toffees as a joke on how British Giles really is on the show, David was given some Tasty Cakes, a videotape of *The King and I*, and other gifts, and Jeff and Sophia were presented with his-and-hers first-aid kits, a pair of handcuffs, and action figures.

Alyson was a favorite with the fans. As Samiel says, "The guys crowded around Aly as thickly as the gals surrounded David." However, Aly was popular with both sexes. Erika was immediately drawn to her: "Alyson was as lovable off-screen as Willow is onscreen. She has a certain presence that draws you to her." She added that Alyson was "exceptionally beautiful. . . . She is truly genuine." In contrast, Keith thought she was very different from Willow, saying, "It may not be apparent without having met her, but Alyson's portrayal of Willow is brilliant, because in person she is confident and dynamic, in contrast to her quiet, reserved character." Tammie agreed that Alyson "is truly a delightful person."

Anthony Stewart Head seemed the most unlike his character. "Tony was stunning," Erika remembers. "He seemed to have the most fun, laughing and offering a smile to everyone. He probably made more hearts melt than Nick and David together." Tony's birthday was six days after the event, so Tammie got everyone at the party to sign a large birthday card for him. As she said, it gave her a great excuse to talk to all of the VIPs, who also signed the card. When the card had been signed by everyone in the room, they began singing "Happy Birthday to You," knowing that Tony was upstairs. He came down, having missed the song entirely, and everyone sang it to him again. Batra remembers that he looked embarrassed, but very touched that everyone did that for him. Everyone thought he was a lot of fun to talk to, and one fan even commented that where she couldn't imagine him before as Frank N. Furter in *The Rocky Horror Picture Show*, she could now picture him in the role easily. Karri described him as a "hippie, a true child of the '60s. He was a trip."

The most popular guest among the people I talked to, though, was Seth Green. He was described as "down-to-earth," "sweet," "the definition of charisma," "a very great guy," and "a cutie." Samiel, who at one point became Seth's unofficial water carrier, says, "Of all the cast, Seth may be my favorite actor, not only for his acting abilities, but also for the kindness he displays." Seth had shown up unexpectedly, and didn't have an official invitation. Karri recalls that AKA Becker, who had made up the invitations, jokingly threatened to kick him out, but promised to send him an official invitation in the mail. A few months later, he ran into Seth in New York, and Seth remembered him and wondered where his invitation was. When AKA Becker told him he still hadn't sent the invitation, Seth jokingly threatened to beat him up.

All night long, Seth met with fans, shook hands and asked what people's real names were. He seemed genuinely excited to be there. One poster said, "If you ever meet him, it will change your thoughts on kids who grow up in the entertainment biz." It was at this party that fans first heard the news that Seth had been signed on as a regular character for the third season. After the excitement surrounding this announcement had died down a little, Erika asked him if he could call her cousin in Oklahoma, who had a Seth Green Web site. Without hesitation he picked up the phone and chatted for about 15 minutes about the site, and after Erika's cousin had explained it to him, he made it the official Seth Green Web site. A few people mentioned how well Aly and Seth got along together, saying you could tell they'd been friends for a long time by the ease with which they spoke to one another.

One of the posting-board members, Marcus, had the foresight to bring a laptop computer and cellular modem with him, which they hooked up to The Bronze. That night the posting board was filled with fans awaiting any news on the PBP, and David, Aly, and Seth all posted their hellos to those who couldn't make the party. Karri got the opportunity to show David the Web site that she has devoted to him, and he was so happy with it that he wanted to sign the guestbook. However, he explained that he was somewhat computer-illiterate, and Karri ended up doing the signing for him. The fans at the PBP also got the five cast members to pose for a photo holding up a sign for the people who couldn't be there. The sign read, "Hi Everybody. I Miss you!!! Posting Board Rules!!!" They then posed for a mock photo of the four guys biting Aly's neck.

The party continued until 1 AM and many of the VIPs stayed very late. Not only did the fans get a rare chance to meet the cast and crew of their favorite television show, but they made a lot of friends among their fellow posting-board members. The cast and crew enjoyed themselves immensely, and as a thank-you RD invited the PBP committee members to the set of *Buffy the Vampire Slayer* a few days later. They got to watch a scene of "I Only Have Eyes for You" as it was being filmed, and they were shown the various sets, such as Buffy's bedroom, her house, The Bronze, and the Sunnydale High cafeteria, which was being built for the episode. In the past, all cafeteria scenes had been shot away from the set, and Joss finally decided to build a cafeteria so the cast and crew wouldn't have to leave the set. One of the people who got to see the sets couldn't believe how real they looked: "Buffy's room was homey, yet it was funny to look out her window and see her roof meeting up with the floor. The Bronze was smaller than it looks on TV but it was still cool. But my favorite was the library. It was just as it looks on TV. Big and booky. It was just so exciting to be in there, to look around and see the millions of scenes they have filmed run through your head."

A chance to meet their idols is something most fans only dream of, but for one evening the dream came true for 100 *Buffy the Vampire Slayer* fans. The crew and the fans worked together to pull off an event that has now become legend among online *Buffy* fans. There is another party planned for 1999, but to find out more information about it, you'll have to log on to the official site and discover for yourself what the posting board is all about.

BUFFY THE VAMPIRE SLAYER EPISODE GUIDE

The following guide contains spoilers for each episode (that is, the entries give away some important plot details), so, if you prefer to be surprised, I recommend you avoid the entries for those episodes you have not yet seen. The episode guide offers background research into some of the demonology to help give the reader a richer understanding of each episode. The opinions expressed in the following pages are mine only, so feel free to disagree. These are intended as reviews of each episode, rather than plot summaries, so you will notice that I often leave out parts of the plot.

At the end of each entry you will find special items of interest. HIGHLIGHT includes one or two things that stood out in the show, but which didn't fit in the summary. NITPICKS are those things that bothered me after watching the episode, but that other people might be able to explain to their satisfaction. OOPS details the bloopers and continuity errors I spotted in the episodes. INTEREST-ING FACT occasionally pops up, listing a tidbit of information about an actor or the show. MUSIC/BANDS lists all the music that was heard in the episode, and for that section I am deeply indebted to Leslie Remencus, who gave me permission to use the information listed on her fabulous *Buffy* music Web site (see Web-site chapter for more details). Finally, BEST POP CULTURE REFERENCE explains a reference that someone in the gang makes in each episode.

SEASON ONE
(MARCH–JUNE 1997)

STARRING: Sarah Michelle Gellar as Buffy Summers
              Anthony Stewart Head as Rupert Giles
              Alyson Hannigan as Willow Rosenberg
              Nicholas Brendon as Xander Harris
              David Boreanaz as Angel
              Charisma Carpenter as Cordelia Chase

1.1 Welcome to the Hellmouth (Part One)

ORIGINAL AIR DATE: March 10, 1997
WRITTEN BY: Joss Whedon
DIRECTED BY: Charles Martin Smith

GUEST CAST: Kristine Sutherland as Joyce Summers
              Ken Lerner as Principal Flutie
              Brian Thompson as Luke
              Eric Balfour as Jesse
              J. Patrick Lawlor as Thomas
              Mark Metcalf as The Master
              Julie Benz as Darla
              Natalie Strauss as Teacher

After being kicked out of her previous school for burning down the gym, Buffy Summers arrives in Sunnydale, only to discover that the high school is built on a hellmouth and she must resume her duties as a vampire slayer.

This pilot episode was excellent! It first aired as a two-hour premiere, but because the two hours are generally rebroadcast separately now, they will be dealt with individually in this episode guide. "Welcome to the Hellmouth" contains all the elements of a good pilot: an introduction to the main characters, background information that lets the viewer know something about what life was like before the story began, a look at the major settings in which the story will take place, all while establishing the main themes of the show.

The episode opens with a brief history of former slayers and where the vampire activity was taking place in the past. It is interesting to note that all the slayers were women, yet the phenomenon of the slayer's gender is never explained on the show. It then moves to a couple of high school kids breaking into the school

Nick, Joss, and Alyson appear at a comic convention.
LISA ROSE

and the viewer is led to believe that a demon of some sort will attack them. Until, of course, one of them turns into a vampire and attacks the other. *Buffy* is a show that will cleverly undercut many of our expectations.

The first trick played on us is that the television show is so different from the movie. While the television Buffy still has the "keen fashion sense" that her original incarnation boasted, she's younger, more sarcastic, more intelligent, and has more personal problems. The movie version of *Buffy the Vampire Slayer* was like *Clueless*, but near the end suddenly tried to be a serious film. The television show carries comedy, action, and drama simultaneously and features a far superior ensemble cast. (The movie is worth seeing, though, if just for Paul Reubens's death scene.)

Alyson Hannigan as Willow is perfect. She's shy, unsure of herself, but incredibly intelligent, and considering that Willow remains consistent in later episodes, it would appear that Hannigan had the role figured out from the start. Giles is great as the *very* British librarian who, as a watcher, knows of his duties but seems completely unprepared for a rebellious slayer (and there isn't a single cup of Taster's Choice in sight!). The way he confidently slams down the *Vampyr* book before an unsuspecting Buffy leads us to think he knows exactly what he is doing, a notion immediately undercut by his surprise when Buffy refuses to pick up the book.

Sarah Michelle Gellar, like Hannigan, seems to know where she's going to take her character this season, so she imbues Buffy with confidence when trying to fit in, annoyance at the thought of slaying vampires, sarcasm with everyone she meets, and an uncertainty that she *should* be the Chosen One.

David Boreanaz is good as Angel, although he doesn't seem as comfortable with the character as he is in later shows. By the episode "Angel," however, he will have polished the character into what we have today. Nicholas as Xander is immediately nerdy, and within moments of making his first appearance he falls (literally) madly in lust with Buffy. In the early episodes his character's self-deprecation becomes somewhat annoying, but, thankfully, that hangup with his manhood (or what he sees as his lack of it) disappears in later episodes. Finally, Charisma is wonderful as that popular girl we all love to hate, and Cordelia is so vicious — while completely oblivious to her own ridiculousness — that you can't help but be intrigued by her. In other words, the ensemble cast is top-notch.

Some of the situations are similar to the pilots of other high school television shows, but Whedon always adds a subtle twist. For example, many shows feature the "enlightened" principal we all wish we had, the guy who's willing to erase the memories of the past and start fresh. However, Principal Flutie rips up Buffy's records before realizing she's burned down her school gym, and spends the rest of the scene frantically taping them together while he lectures her on responsibility. This scene is hilarious, establishing Principal Flutie as one of the funniest characters in the early episodes.

An interesting aspect of this initial episode is that at the very beginning, when Buffy is having one of her prophetic dreams, we see snippets of the rest of the first season — the *Vampyr* book, cemeteries, blood, candles, Angel's cross, Moloch, vampires — establishing the themes to come. Among those themes is Whedon's vision of high school: the students are not all "Ra! Ra! Go, Sunnydale!" but share a quiet angst and can't wait to get out of there. Cordelia is the popular girl, yet she's intelligent and quick-witted, often putting even our sarcastic slayerettes to shame. Although Cordelia accepts Buffy into her fold because Buffy's from Los Angeles, Buffy quickly realizes that although she was popular in LA, being a slayer is going to change everything here in Sunnydale.

Whereas the *Buffy* movie only touched on the idea that slaying would seriously interfere with a teenager's life, this theme becomes the major focus of the show. Buffy returns to the library after seeing a dead victim of a vampire and tells Giles that she's retired and no longer wants to be a slayer. She pleads that she just wants to be normal, but Giles senses that an apocalypse is coming. Buffy surrenders to her sense of duty, but does not take her job as seriously as Giles would like her to. At The Bronze — which, as a setting, is a great idea and an amazing-looking club — Giles tells her to hone in on possible vampires. Instead of honing in, however, Buffy simply points to a guy who is dressed in the New Romantic style of the 1980s and fingers him as a vampire. After all, a vampire wouldn't necessarily be in tune with the latest fashion trends. Funnily enough, her instincts are correct. So although Buffy might not have the book smarts or knowledge of history that Giles thinks is necessary in a slayer, she and her friends will rely on their in-depth knowledge and awareness of the society around them to survive.

"Welcome to the Hellmouth" was a great introduction to the series, although newcomers should watch this and the next episode together for a fuller effect.

HIGHLIGHT: The "coolness test" that Cordelia makes Buffy take (allowing her to skip the written).

NITPICKS: This nitpick is moving ahead to the end of Season Two, where we discover that by the time Buffy moves to Sunnydale, Angel has been following her for a while. In the pilot, when he first meets her, he says, "I thought you'd be taller." If he'd been following her for over a year, wouldn't he know how tall she is? Also, I have two major nitpicks that apply to the whole series. First of all, why is it that not a single recurring character on this show has a sibling? The high school years often bring out tension, antagonism, and friendship between siblings, yet Joss has opted to avoid the possibilities that siblings could create. Just imagine Willow trying to keep Buffy's secret from a younger sister. The other nitpick is that when the vampires suck the blood from their victims' necks there isn't a single drop of blood on the demons' mouths. I realize the show is meant for younger viewers, but this discrepancy is a little unbelievable.

OOPS: When Buffy follows the vampire into the back of The Bronze, she breaks off the leg of a stool to use as a weapon. When she raises it up to Cordelia, it's been perfectly chiseled into a stake.

INTERESTING FACT: Ken Lerner appeared in an episode of *Happy Days* as a bully, Rocko Malachi, who picked on Richie Cunningham. Also, Joss has admitted to basing certain characters on real-life people — Cordelia is named after a cruel girl with whom his wife attended high school, and Xander is modeled after Joss himself.

BEST POP CULTURE REFERENCE: Right before Buffy stakes Thomas, she says to him, "Okay, first of all, what's with the outfit? Live in the now, okay? You look like DeBarge!" DeBarge were a 1980s family pop group with hits like "Rhythm of the Night," "Who's Holding Donna Now?" and "You Wear It Well." Admittedly, their outfits were pretty flashy.

MUSIC/BANDS: The *Buffy* theme is written and performed by Nerf Herder, but is not yet available on CD. When Buffy is trying to decide what to wear to The Bronze, the song in the background is "Saturated" by Sprung Monkey. When Buffy enters The Bronze for the first time, Sprung Monkey is playing "Believe" onstage, and later they play "Swirl." As Buffy leaves The Bronze looking for Willow, they're playing "Things Are Changing." All of these songs are on their CD, *Swirl*. The scores for the first-season episodes were written by Walter Murphy.

1.2 The Harvest

ORIGINAL AIR DATE: March 10, 1997
WRITTEN BY: Joss Whedon
DIRECTED BY: John T. Kretchmer

GUEST CAST (who weren't in Part One):
         Mercedes McNab as Harmony
         Jeffrey Steven Smith as Guy in Computer Class
         Teddy Lane, Jr. as Bouncer
         Deborah Brown as Girl

When Giles discovers that The Master is about to be set free through his vessel, Luke, Buffy must try to stop the harvest before it begins.

The second half of the pilot focuses less on the characters and more on the vampires. We learn that many of the vampires have been with the Master for centuries, but the Master has been trapped in a church that, during an earthquake in 1937, was swallowed underground, taking him with it. When Jessie, a friend of Xander and Willow, goes missing, we learn something of Whedon's vampire mythology: A vampire is actually a demon inhabiting the lifeless body of the person it attacked. The demon takes on the look and personality of the former owner of the body, but it's all part of the trick. In other words, becoming a vampire is more of a demonic possession than a transformation. Notice how easily Buffy and Giles explain that Jessie is no longer Jessie but a demon, yet later, when the question is whether or not Angel should be destroyed, they won't be so quick to make the same rationalization.

The Master ordains Luke as his "vessel" in a strange perversion of a Christian baptism ceremony. Instead of placing a cross of holy water on the baptised's forehead, the Master draws a symbol similar to a Mercedes-Benz logo in blood (which opens a myriad of possible interpretations, but let's leave that one alone). The fact that this hellish activity is happening in a church gives the writers the perfect opportunity to set up the scenes as reversals of Christian ceremonies. Later, the Master will preach to the "Anointed" as if he is a member of his hellish congregation.

Darla is a wonderful character — a female vampire who is deceivingly cute. As we will later discover, in each era she chooses an outfit by which men will be drawn to her. In the eighteenth century, she wore the dress of a noblewoman, for example, and in the 1930s she wore a kimono. However, it is disturbing that the outfit she chooses for the late twentieth century is a private school-girl's uniform — let's hope it's simply Darla taking advantage of the fact that her main targets are now high school boys. Despite the prominence of male vampires in vampire fiction, Darla is the first vampire to kill in this television series.

Buffy's mother is a major figure on the show — as is typical with many television series aimed at a high-school-aged audience — and she's very different from her movie counterpart. In the *Buffy the Vampire Slayer* movie, Buffy's parents are flighty and stupid people who are never around, making it difficult to believe in them as real characters. However, in the show, Buffy's parents are divorced, she only sees her father on occasional weekends, and her mother is an intelligent woman who can't seem to connect with her 16-year-old daughter. One of the best and most hilarious moments in this episode occurs when Buffy is grabbing her tools of destruction to halt the apocalypse and Joyce enters her bedroom to tell her she cannot go out that night. Joyce thinks she's talking to a typical teenager, not aware of the serious duty her daughter must perform, and sighs, "Everything is life and death when you're a 16-year-old!" She assures Buffy that if she doesn't go out it won't be the end of the world, not realizing the irony of her own words.

The action scenes at the end of the episode are amazing, and while Sarah Michelle Gellar does have a stunt double, you'd never know it — the editing is seamless. Not only is Buffy physically strong, but she uses her wits to overcome her opponent, weakening Luke by making him think he would be burned by sunlight. Even Angel is impressed when she averts Armageddon.

Now, you'd think a bunch of vampires with disfigured faces feeding on club kids and getting beat up by a sophomore girl would have some impact on the other high school students, but we find out that things aren't that complicated in Sunnydale. As Giles explains, "People rationalize what they can and forget what they can't." In this case, Cordelia explains to her friends that the fiasco at the club was caused by rival gangs. And so life continues as usual at peaceful Sunnydale High, where a giant hellmouth waits below the surface to open and devour them all.

HIGHLIGHT: Willow tricking Cordelia into deleting her computer assignment.

NITPICKS: In this episode, Buffy leaps over the school gate and jumps down from the rafters at The Bronze, yet later in Season Two, she'll appear to lack these superhuman skills.

OOPS: In many instances on this show, vampires get burned but it leaves no scars. In this episode Darla has holy water thrown in her face, but the next time we see her there is no evidence of it. In "Angel," Buffy's cross will burn an impression into his chest, but it will be gone the next time we see him, and in "What's My Line? Part Two," Drusilla will torture Angel with holy water, but again it will leave no scars. Yet at the end of "WML2," Spike's face will be burned, and he'll be scarred for the next few episodes. Also, Cordelia tells Harmony she's going to The Bronze because it's Friday night and there's no cover, yet there is a cover (you can see people paying the bouncer at the door) and everyone's back at school the next day.

INTERESTING FACT: When this episode first aired as the second half of part one, the WB broadcast a Ford commercial starring Susan Lucci. Hmm . . . looks like Kendall's outdoing her mom.

MUSIC/BANDS: As Buffy talks with Principal Flutie at the gate, the song playing in the background is "Right My Wrong," by Sprung Monkey. At The Bronze, Cordelia exclaims, "Ooh! I love this song!" referring to "Wearing Me Down" by the Dashboard Prophets. As the vampires approach The Bronze for the harvest, "Ballad for My Dead Friends," also by Dashboard Prophets, is playing and continues into the action scenes. Both songs are on their *Burning Out the Inside* CD.

BEST POP CULTURE REFERENCE: Buffy tells the gang to watch the exits and that she'll handle the vampires, adding, "Don't go Wild Bunch on me." *The Wild Bunch* is a 1969 Sam Peckinpah movie, and at the time was the bloodiest, goriest movie ever. Set in Mexico in 1913, it's a Western about a group of violent men who see the age of cowboys coming to an end. Despite an inherent code of honor that both they and the officials hunting them seem to follow, they are eventually pushed too far and invite an all-out massacre on a Mexican town. *The Wild Bunch* is an amazing movie and, not surprisingly, was apparently a big influence on Joss Whedon. The head of the bunch is Pike, the name of Luke Perry's character in the *Buffy the Vampire Slayer* movie, and another member of the bunch is named Angel, who, being Mexican himself, ends up caught between his gang and his people. It wasn't a coincidence that Joss gave Angel that name. (See also "Bad Eggs.")

1.3 The Witch

ORIGINAL AIR DATE: March 17, 1997
WRITTEN BY: Dana Reston
DIRECTED BY: Stephen Cragg

GUEST CAST: Elizabeth Anne Allen as Amy Madison
Robin Riker as Catherine the Great
Kristine Sutherland as Joyce Summers
Jim Doughan as Mr. Pole
Nicole Prescott as Lishanne
Amanda Wilmshurst as Senior Cheerleader
William Monaghan as Dr. Gregory

When members of the cheerleading team are felled by strange illnesses, the gang guesses that a witch is casting spells on them.

When we think of witches, we tend to think of the infamous witch trials in Europe and America, particularly those in Salem, Massachusetts. The witch hunt in Europe was initially sparked by the church — both the Catholic church, and especially (after the Reformation) the various Protestant churches. Although its beginnings in different forms stretched back to the fourteenth or fifteenth centuries, the hunt reached its peak a couple of centuries later. Scholars have had differing opinions on how widespread the slaughter was, and estimates of the number of deaths have ranged anywhere between 100,000 and nine million. If accused of witchcraft, a person would rarely escape execution or imprisonment. It's also surprising to discover that many children were put to death as accused witches. However, most of those charged with witchcraft were adults who were outcasts of society — generally peasants who did not attend church — and their deaths led to a countryside filled with starving beggar children.

Germany probably had more witch trials than any other country, but the most notorious witch trials were held in Salem, Massachusetts, in 1692. These were different from their European counterparts in that most of the accused were Puritan churchgoers who had always been useful members of society. A group of girls began saying that they'd been possessed by the devil, and that they could identify the witches in their village. During the trials they would go into convulsions, claim possession, and point out people in the courts as witches. Why these girls acted in such a manner is not known, although some scholars have speculated that their actions arose from being stifled in every way by an overly strict society. At the end of one year, two dozen people had been executed and over 150 imprisoned.

Today, witches exist as pagan lovers of nature who belong to a religion called Wicca, begun in 1951 by Gerald Gardner. Many witches perform good magic, or white magic, which promotes healing and gives strength to its recipients. Witches and other pagans follow three important principles: embrace love and a kinship with Nature; follow the pagan ethic, which is, "Do what thou will, but harm none"; accept the presence of both god and goddess, without considering one gender superior to the other. Witches who perform black magic, or evil magic that aims to harm, are shunned by others in the religion. All magic follows the Law of Threefold Return — pagans believe that any act of magic will rebound on the magician threefold, meaning if a witch performs black magic, he or she will experience a negative impact with three times the force of the act performed.

In "The Witch," the writers do a great job tricking the viewer into believing Amy is the witch. The real topic of this episode, though, is the often precarious relationships between teenagers and their parents. Buffy tries to reach out to her mother, but Joyce is too caught up in her work to notice. When she, in turn, attempts to connect with her daughter, Buffy accuses her mother of trying to mold her into a miniature Joyce. The tension between Buffy and Joyce is caused by Buffy's envy of the relationship between Amy and her mother, which, unknown to Buffy, is actually violent and abusive.

Robin Riker, as Catherine the Great, is superb when playing the part of a teenager trapped in an adult body. She's jittery, the way Amy was at the beginning, making the two roles appear seamless. The scene where Amy (in her mother's body) tells Buffy what happened would have been more realistic if she'd said her mother had switched their bodies a couple of days before. Instead, she says the bodies had been switched a few months before, meaning the poor, dejected girl at the beginning of the episode was Amy's mother. However, it would explain how the first cheerleader caught on fire.

The fact that Buffy wants to be a cheerleader links her to the movie Buffy, and Giles is like Merrick (the movie Buffy's watcher) in that he doesn't want Buffy to join. He calls cheerleading a cult and forbids her from trying out, but Buffy won't listen to him. Speaking of Giles, we see how excited he is to be living on the hellmouth when he looks happy to hear about the cheerleader who catches on fire. "That's the thrill of living on the hellmouth," he says with an expression of glee, prompting surprised looks on the faces of the others.

Willow is a great character in this episode. Xander tells her how he feels about Buffy, and Willow's caught between her feelings for him and her friendship with both him and Buffy. When he gives Buffy a bracelet that reads, "Yours always," the hurt look on Willow's face speaks volumes, yet she doesn't hold it against Buffy or Xander. This is also the episode where Xander calls Willow his "guy friend" who knows how women feel, but Willow has a look of triumph on her face when Buffy calls Xander her girl friend. Willow and Xander also take a more active role in Buffy's slaying, calling themselves the slayerettes, and Willow's strength comes through when she attempts to stall Amy's mother by standing in her way and asking, "Do you actually *ride* a broom?"

On seeing this episode for the first time, one might be surprised — where are the vampires? However, as a metaphor for the pressure parents put on their teenaged children, it is nonetheless a lot of fun.

HIGHLIGHT: Buffy's rendition of "Macho Man."

NITPICKS: How did Amy get Buffy's bracelet?

MUSIC/BANDS: During Amber's dance routine and when the Razorbacks head out onto the basketball court, the song playing is "Twilight Zone" by 2 Unlimited, from their CD *Get Ready For This*.

BEST POP CULTURE REFERENCE: After Buffy administers the quicksilver test on Amy, she tells the others, "The test was positive. She's our Sabrina," a reference to the current television show *Sabrina the Teenage Witch*, which is a spinoff of the Archie Comics character.

1.4 Teacher's Pet

ORIGINAL AIR DATE: March 25, 1997
WRITTEN BY: David Greenwalt
DIRECTED BY: Bruce Seth Green

GUEST CAST: Ken Lerner as Principal Flutie
Musetta Vander as Nathalie French
Jean Speegle Howard as the *real* Nathalie French
Jackson Price as Blaine
Jack Knight as Homeless Guy
Michael Ross Verona as Teacher
Karim Oliver as Bud #1

Xander develops an infatuation for his biology teacher, not realizing she's a giant praying mantis in disguise.

"Teacher's Pet" takes the focus off Buffy and places it on Xander. For the first time we can truly understand his anxieties about his own masculinity. After all, he's in love with a girl who always ends up protecting him and getting him out of sticky situations. This episode opens with a dream sequence where Xander fights off vampires to save a helpless Buffy, who adores him, only to jump up onstage and resume his position as lead guitarist in a rock band. While the daydream is very funny, it's also poignant, for we must understand that as exciting as it is for women to see other women defending themselves, it must be difficult for a male who is raised in a society where he is supposed to be the hero and the female the damsel in distress. We also discover Buffy has a thing for Angel. Interestingly, he shows up to warn her about a man with big claws (an obvious allusion to Freddie Krueger) who will eventually be used to vanquish the bigger problem — the praying mantis who preys on virgins.

The idea of a high school guy being devoured by a praying mantis as a metaphor for losing his virginity is very clever. Women often complain about society's double standard toward sexuality — women must remain virgins, while men are expected to have made several "conquests" by the time they've graduated high school. But what kind of pressure does that expectation put on a guy? In "Teacher's Pet," Blaine buys into the stereotype but gets around his situation by being a good actor. A member of the varsity championship football team, Blaine can easily convince others that he's slept with several girls. Xander, on the other hand, tries the same schtick but falls flat on his face. While Willow expresses her admiration for both of them remaining virgins, Buffy buys into the double standard, acting with shock upon realizing Xander is a virgin.

Enter Nathalie French. A beautiful woman who pretends to fall for Xander, she presents him with the opportunity not only to lose his virginity, but to do so with an older woman. Ms. French is symbolic of what society's expectations do to men — perhaps many lose their virginity against their better judgment simply to cater to that pressure. To make the metaphor even more explicit, Xander and Blaine are literally locked in cages, looking out at a creature who wants to use them only to fertilize her eggs and will kill them in the process. Xander, who will be her first prey, listens as Blaine recounts the mating procedure with grim horror. Perhaps this is also symbolic of the reaction many teenage boys have to the realities of sex.

But why a praying mantis? The obvious reasons to choose such a creature are made clear in the episode — the female praying mantis often bites off the head of the male during mating, then eats the rest of him when she's finished. Also, the Greeks believed the mantis had supernatural powers because of the way it folds its front legs and looks up, as if praying. An important aspect of the mantis that isn't broached in the episode is its ability to blend into its surroundings. The mantis is the same color as the leaves of the trees it inhabits, and is therefore camouflaged, hidden from its prey. Similarly, Ms. French is "camouflaged" as a substitute teacher, and the boys have no idea how dangerous she is. Also, a mantis can only eat live insects, hence Ms. French's cricket sandwich.

While this episode was clearly focused on Xander and his anxieties about his manliness, we are also given a glance at Buffy's insecurity about herself. Dr. Gregory becomes an important person to her because he believes in her — not a single other person outside of the gang believes unconditionally that she can succeed. Even Buffy's mother constantly brings up her past to remind her of her shortcomings. When Dr. Gregory is killed, Buffy is left alone, having to prove herself by starting at square one.

On the surface, "Teacher's Pet" isn't as funny or interesting as other episodes, but it is far more clever than it appears to be.

HIGHLIGHT: Principal Flutie lecturing Buffy on the importance of healing.

NITPICKS: Why were Dr. Gregory's glasses still on the front desk at the end of the episode? If they'd been cracked in the struggle, wouldn't the police have taken them as evidence? Also, when Buffy is hunting the "claw guy," why does she climb the fence? Can't she just jump over? And couldn't Angel have been a little more specific when warning Buffy about him?

MUSIC/BANDS: When Xander walks into The Bronze the band onstage is Superfine, performing "Already Met You." When he smashes the mantis eggs, the song is "Stoner Love." Both are from Superfine's vinyl record, *Stoner Love*.

BEST POP CULTURE REFERENCE: After Buffy sees Ms. French turn her neck 180 degrees, she tells Willow, "No, I'm not saying she craned her neck; we're talking full-on *Exorcist* twist." William Friedkin's *The Exorcist* was a 1973 horror film starring Linda Blair as Regan, a girl believed to be possessed by the devil. In one shocking scene, Regan rotates her head all the way around. This episode was also clearly influenced by Mike Nichols's 1967 classic *The Graduate*, starring Dustin Hoffman.

1.5 Never Kill a Boy on the First Date

ORIGINAL AIR DATE: March 31, 1997
WRITTEN BY: Rob Des Hotel and Dean Batali
DIRECTED BY: David Semel

GUEST CAST: Mark Metcalf as The Master
Andrew J. Ferchland as Colin/The Anointed One
Geoff Meed as Andrew Borber
Christopher Wiehl as Owen
Paul-Felix Montez as Mysterious Guy
Robert Mont as Van Driver

When Buffy catches the eye of a really cute high school guy, she quickly learns how being a slayer interferes with having a normal life.

The vampires are back, and the Master is still plotting a way to escape his underground prison. We learn of a new twist on the ol' Master/slayer prophecy — the coming of the Anointed One, who will lead Buffy into Hell. Giles conveniently discovers the prophecy at the same time, and the rest of the episode is spent trying to figure out which of the people who die in a bus/vampire accident has become the Anointed.

As far as the chemistry among the ensemble cast, this episode develops the relationship between Buffy and Giles — he seems more relaxed around her now, while coming to an understanding that Buffy will undergo personal difficulties he hadn't anticipated. When Owen first arrives in the library, Buffy goes into cute flirt mode while Giles is curt with him. Buffy must remind Giles that a library is a place where people take out books, yet so far they've never been interrupted (apparently Sunnydale High doesn't boast a lot of readers). Buffy is trapped between her duty as the Chosen One and her overwhelming desire to have a real life, while Giles is caught between his duty to mankind — training and disciplining the slayer — and the fact that he cares about her. When she begs Giles to let her go on a date with Owen, he stresses that her "fantasies" must be put on hold for the good of mankind. However, what she must explain to him is that at 16, a date with a good-looking guy seems more important than the fate of humanity.

Perhaps because of his new understanding of Buffy's situation, Giles does not put his foot down to tell her she must stop the Anointed, and she goes to The Bronze with Owen. Giles is almost killed, Willow and Xander must lure Buffy back to save him, and Owen steps in to play the hero, almost getting killed himself. In one catastrophic evening, Buffy is forced to realize that she will never have a normal life, and that having a boyfriend will only endanger his life. Giles comes to an understanding as well, and for the first time becomes a father figure in Buffy's life, explaining to her that when he was informed he would be the watcher he was told of the sacrifices he'd have to make. Unfortunately, no one seriously explained things to Buffy until this point.

The dialogue in this episode is top-notch, and in the span of one hour Buffy and Giles move from sarcasm to empathy. At the beginning, when Giles reminds Buffy of the serious consequences of telling people she is the slayer, she reassures him that she won't wear her button that reads, "I'm a slayer — Ask me how!" And when Buffy begs Giles to let her have the night off for a date, he sardonically replies that he'll go back in time and ask the demon prophets to please put off the apocalypse for a day so Buffy can have a life. Yet, by the end, Giles realizes how serious that date was to Buffy, and Buffy realizes Giles was right that she must take her duty more seriously.

This episode was very well done, and its repercussions will be echoing in episodes to come.

HIGHLIGHT: Owen's reaction to seeing Giles at Buffy's house in the evening: "Wow, you really care about your work!"

NITPICKS: The writers should come up with a more detailed and specific history of past slayers and watchers. Previous slayers are all women, yet Giles mentions his grandmother was a watcher. Is it a hereditary thing? Why was his family chosen as watchers?

MUSIC/BANDS: The band at The Bronze is Velvet Chain, performing "Strong" as Buffy and Owen walk out to the dance floor, and "Treason" as they leave the floor to walk to the stairs. Both songs are from the band's *Groovy Side* CD. Cordelia and Owen dance to "Rotten Apple" by Three Day Wheely, from their *Rubber Halo* CD, and when Angel comes to warn Buffy about the impending disaster, the song is "Junky Girl" by Rubber, from their self-titled CD. Finally, during Buffy's last talk with Owen, the song in the background is "Let the Sun Fall Down" by Kim Richey, from her self-titled CD.

BEST POP CULTURE REFERENCE: Buffy drops her tray in the cafeteria after Xander tries to guess what the green stuff on the plate was, and Owen says, "At least you don't have to eat your soylent green." This is a reference to the 1973 sci-fi classic, *Soylent Green*, starring Charlton Heston. In the year 2022, Earth's food supply has been all but depleted, so the government manufactures something called soylent green to feed to the masses. Heston's character, Detective Thorn, is suspicious and investigates to find out what soylent green really is and how the government is making it. At the end, he makes his terrible discovery, leading to the now classic and oft-repeated line, "Soylent green is people!"

1.6 The Pack

ORIGINAL AIR DATE: April 7, 1997
WRITTEN BY: Matt Kiene and Joe Reinkemeyer
DIRECTED BY: Bruce Seth Green

GUEST CAST: Ken Lerner as Principal Flutie
Eion Bailey as Kyle
Jeff Maynard as Lance

Brian Gross as Tor
Jennifer Sky as Heidi
Michael McRaine as Rhonda
James Stephens as Zookeeper
David Brisbin as Mr. Anderson
Barbara K. Whinnery as Mrs. Anderson
Gregory White as Coach Herrold

Xander and four bullies become possessed by a hyena and begin attacking people.

"The Pack" focuses on school bullies and how cruel and thoughtless high school kids can be. On a school trip to the zoo (don't bullies always strike on school trips?), Buffy is mocked by a group of four bullies and later tells Xander and Willow how much she hates school trips.

After chasing a kid into the hyena exhibit, Xander and the bullies become possessed. We later find out that possession can happen during a predatory act — the bullies fall under the spell for chasing Lance, and Xander succumbs because he was chasing the bullies. Like the "cool kids" at school, the five maintain a pack mentality throughout the episode, always tracking down a member if he or she goes missing. The legend of a hyena learning a person's name to lure them away parallels bullies and their prey — they learn the names of their victims, trick them into thinking they'll make them part of their group, and then pick on that person ceaselessly, as happens with Lance. The addition of dodge ball is brilliant; the mere mention of that barbaric "sport" is enough to send shivers down anyone's spine if they've been on the bad end of a game.

The fact that the cruel behavior of the possessed mirrors much of the bully activity in schools leads Giles to think everything is normal. He points out the three main traits of the "animal" behavior that Buffy has mentioned — picking on the weak; changing clothing and attitude; spending all spare time "lounging with imbeciles" — and understandably diagnoses Xander as a normal teenager. His sarcastic comment to Buffy, "Of course, you'll have to kill him," is wickedly funny in this situation. Buffy, however, knows something is wrong, not because of the others — their behavior is consistent with how they were before — but because of Xander. When he tells Willow he won't have to look at her "pasty face" any longer, he is acting out Willow's nightmare, and her face fills with horror. Hannigan is excellent in this scene.

Although the main theme of this episode focuses on bully activity in school, it also touches on another issue — date rape. Xander tries to rape Buffy, telling her she wants it because he's now dangerous and mean like Angel. Had she not been the slayer, she probably wouldn't have made it out of the situation, but she does. This scene is subtle and handled well.

It was reassuring to see that the first thing Xander did when the possession wore off was to save Willow, and also that Willow is mature enough to recognize that Xander acting like an animal is not really Xander. However, the ending could leave viewers a little uncertain of their relationship. If Xander trying to rape Buffy was him acting out a tendency that stems from a genuine desire for her, then was his treatment of Willow in any way based on reality? Was he speaking his mind? Also, Giles states that he can't find any mention in his reading on animal possession about amnesia afterward, and he's right. Yet, notice later in "Phases" how everyone accepts that Oz can't remember what he does while he's a werewolf.

Sadly, this episode was our goodbye to Principal Flutie, who was an absolutely hilarious character. It was such a shock to see the death of a fairly prominent character on the show, but exciting at the same time, for now we know how unpredictable this show will be. Ah, Principal Flutie . . . we hardly knew ye.

HIGHLIGHT: Willow's reaction to zebras mating: "It's like the Heimlich . . . with stripes!"

NITPICKS: Why is Buffy the only girl in gym class wearing a top with spaghetti straps? It seemed like an obvious ploy to make the lead actress stand out.

MUSIC/BANDS: When Xander is first acting strangely around Willow and Buffy at The Bronze, the song playing is "All You Want" by the Dashboard Prophets, and when Kyle and his friends enter The Bronze, it's "Reluctant Man" by Sprung Monkey. One of the best uses of music on the show is during the slow-motion sequence when Xander and the pack are walking around the Sunnydale campus: the song is "Job's Eyes" by Far, from their CD *Tin Cans and Strings for You*.

BEST POP CULTURE REFERENCE: When Giles is trying to rationalize Xander's strange behavior, Buffy exclaims, "I can't believe you of all people are trying to Scully me!" One of the biggest running jokes among *X-Files* fans is that after five seasons of seeing paranormal activity, spaceships, apparent aliens in bottles, etc., Dana Scully *still* attempts to rationalize every strange occurrence, refusing to believe that something is out there.

ORIGINAL AIR DATE: April 14, 1997
WRITTEN BY: David Greenwalt
DIRECTED BY: Scott Brazil

GUEST CAST: Mark Metcalf as The Master
Kristine Sutherland as Joyce Summers
Julie Benz as Darla
Charles Wesley as Meanest Vamp
Andrew J. Ferchland as The Anointed One

Buffy finally admits her feelings for Angel, only to discover he's a vampire.

"Angel" was a great episode and probably the one that is most important to the second season. It opens with Buffy telling Willow how much she's fallen for Angel, yet she's never acted very interested in him before. Has she just been thinking about him more lately? It must be difficult for Willow, knowing that Buffy's feelings for Angel are much like her own feelings for Xander, yet Buffy has more of a chance with her crush than Willow does with hers.

We again see the Master, who now sends out The Three — three warriors stemming back to the mythology books who can take on anything and anybody. As exciting as the fight scene with Buffy is, The Three probably would have annihilated her and Angel pretty quickly, if their reputations reflect reality. However, Angel saves Buffy (as he does many times) and the Master is foiled once again. The Anointed is being taught things by the Master, but you'd think the kid would begin to question the power of these vampires after realizing none of them can kill the slayer.

Angel's first kiss with Buffy, where he accidentally transforms into a vampire, was an exciting one, but probably something many viewers foresaw. How else would Angel have known everything about the vampires? It certainly explains why he doesn't stay around for very long. We find out a lot of new information in this episode — Angel is 241 years old; he used to be the most vicious of vampires; a gypsy curse has left him with a conscience; he is a vampire who refuses to kill people. His face transforms when he gets angry, but the feelings he has for Buffy are probably ones he hasn't felt in a long time, so he transforms by accident (perhaps a metaphor for what happens to teenage boys when they get excited?). Buffy screams for the first time — she's used to seeing vampires, but not to having friends turn into them.

As if vampire slaying wasn't terrible enough for a 16-year-old

girl, she now must face that her boyfriend is a vampire. Xander —
who will always be rather insensitive to Buffy when it comes to
Angel — tells Buffy she has to kill him. Giles does it with more
sensitivity, explaining as he did in the pilot when he was talking
about Jessie that a vampire takes on a person's personality and
appearance but that that person is dead. With Angel, however, this
rationale isn't so clear: if Angel possesses his soul, does that mean
the demon has not killed him, but instead inhabits the body *with*
him? Or is Angel really dead, and by imbuing him with a soul, the
gypsies gave the *demon* a conscience? If everyone else is having
problems trying to figure out what's going on, imagine what Buffy
must be dealing with! The feelings she has for Angel are problematic,
and always will be, and in a later episode she'll wish she'd killed
him when she had the chance. But what if she had? Would she have
been able to live with herself, not realizing what was really going
to happen with him?

Meanwhile, Angel is going through a personal battle of his own,
with no help from Darla. Darla was Angel's lover for centuries, and
now that she senses his feelings for Buffy, she must remind him why
he can't be with her. How do you date a person when you don't eat
anything but blood, you can't stand sunlight, you have to be on guard
constantly for fear you'll lose control and kill her, and you're over
two centuries old? So, just as Giles, Xander, and Willow are reasoning with Buffy that she can't date a vampire, Darla is reasoning with
Angel that he can't date a mortal. When Darla tricks Buffy into
believing that Angel attacked her mother, what is most disturbing
is the way Angel longingly gazes at the wound on Joyce's neck.

"Angel" cleverly demonstrates how most relationships work —
outside forces like family and friends impose their values and
opinions on the individuals who are in the relationships, not allowing them to work out their differences on their own. Here, those
outside forces pressure Buffy and Angel to face off against one
another, and they both realize that neither can kill the other.

This episode was the first time Buffy was trained to use weapons
other than stakes. She uses a staff, and immediately graduates to
crossbow, which we will see her use again in "Prophecy Girl." We
also hear mention of Buffy's diary, begging the question, does she
keep a diary because she is the slayer or because she's a 16-year-old
girl? Giles often mentions the watcher diaries, but there is no
mention of past slayer diaries.

This was well written and beautifully acted. Boreanaz knows what
he's doing with Angel, and rewatching "Angel" after seeing the
second season shows us how these early episodes already contained

EVERETT COLLECTION/WARNER BROS.

hints about what happens in the future. The ending, where Buffy and Angel agree their relationship won't work, is very poignant, as is the burn that Buffy's cross leaves in Angel's skin.

HIGHLIGHT: The cockroach fumigation party.

NITPICKS: When Giles realizes it was Darla who bit Joyce, not Angel, he immediately leaves the hospital to stop Buffy from killing Angel. Why? Angel is still a vampire, isn't he? Also, if Darla was the Master's "favorite" for 400 years, why didn't he act more favorably toward her?

OOPS: When Angel explains to Buffy how his soul was returned to him, he says he killed a gypsy girl in the Romani clan. It was the Kalderash clan; Romani is the gypsy language, not the name of a tribe.

MUSIC/BANDS: As Buffy and Angel say goodbye at the end of the episode, the song playing is the appropriately titled "I'll Remember You" by Sophie Zelmani, from her self-titled CD.

BEST POP CULTURE REFERENCE: The scene in which Darla is on her back on the pool table shooting at Buffy is borrowed from similar scenes in several John Woo films. In particular, action hero Chow Yun Fat shoots two guns while lying on his back in the films *The Killer* and *Hard-Boiled*, and John Travolta does it in *Face/Off*.

1.8 I Robot, You Jane

ORIGINAL AIR DATE: April 28, 1997
WRITTEN BY: Ashley Gable and Thomas A. Swyden
DIRECTED BY: Stephen Posey

GUEST CAST: Robia LaMorte as Jenny Calendar
Jamison Ryan as Fritz
Mark Deakins as Malcolm/Moloch (voice)
Chad Lindberg as Dave
Pierrino Mascarino as Thelonius
Edith Fields as School Nurse
Damon Sharp as Male Student

Willow falls for a guy she meets on the Internet, not realizing he is actually a pagan demon who is taking over the world through its computer systems.

"I Robot, You Jane" is probably the most over-the-top episode in the first season, and the appearance of the robot at the end will have more than one viewer moaning, "Oh, puh-leeze!" However, the use of Moloch as the demon is an intelligent move, for he was one of the most feared of the pagan deities.

It is believed that the origin of the cult that worshipped Moloch is Canaanite, for when his name appears in the Bible it is in reference to the Canaanites. Moloch's worshippers would sacrifice their children — often the first-born — to him. In Leviticus 18:21, God explicitly forbids the Jews to follow this practice: "Do not hand over any of your children to be used in the worship of the god Moloch, because that would bring disgrace on the name of God, the LORD." Later, it is mentioned that King Ahaz and King Manasseh of Judah sacrifice their sons to him, and in 2 Kings 23:10, King Josiah destroys Moloch's temple to put a stop to the human sacrifice.

Students of English literature will recognize Moloch as one of Satan's minions in *Paradise Lost*. When Satan battled against Heaven, Moloch was the strongest fighter, and when Satan's followers are listed in Book One, Moloch is the first to be named:

> First Moloch, horrid King besmear'd with blood
> Of human sacrifice, and parents' tears
> Though for the noise of Drums and Timbrels loud
> Their children's cries unheard, that pass'd through fire,
> To his grim Idol. (1.392–396)

Later, when Satan organizes his hellish council and asks his devils whether or not they should wage war on Heaven, it is Moloch, the general-in-chief of Satan's army, who first speaks, urging them to go to war, reasoning that the worst that could happen is death, which is better than being trapped in Hell.

It is fitting that *Buffy the Vampire Slayer*'s writers should allude to *Paradise Lost*, because the plight of the Master is similar to that of Satan. For revolting against Heaven, Satan and the angels who supported him are sent to Hell, a horrible underground pit of fire where they plot how to escape to fight God's army once again. Similarly, the Master and his followers are trapped underground, although the vampires have a way of going above temporarily. Many of the Master's speeches are strikingly similar to Satan's as well.

A disturbing element of this episode is the allusions — intended or not — to Nazi Germany. Moloch seems like Hitler reincarnated, and his various levels of control mirror Hitler's power over Germany in the 1930s and '40s. Moloch is a leader who tells his followers he loves them, but when they return that love and trust he kills them. The Internet seems like a positive wave of the future — as Naziism was to many — but when something goes wrong they realize how potentially dangerous it is, and by then it's too late. One of the computer hackers who does Moloch's dirty work is named Fritz, the term the Allied forces used for German soldiers. Moloch is the god of human sacrifice; Buffy is almost killed in a shower; Buffy and Xander become trapped in a gas chamber. And if these references were too subtle, the writers make a more obvious allusion when Moloch changes the thesis of a student's paper to read, "Nazi Germany was a model of a well-ordered society." The parallels are interesting, but the writers' intentions are unclear. Was there a reason to make reference to Hitler?

There were a few inconsistences with how the computers worked in the show. When Buffy is trying to find Willow's file to delete it, she types it in the file finder program. Yet, if you look closely, the file was on the desktop to begin with. Willow doesn't question the fact that her home computer tells her she has mail when she wasn't even online — the modem must be active for her computer to detect mail. When Malcolm is skimming the principal's records to glean information on Buffy, they wouldn't be showing on the principal's screen. If Moloch is accessing the information from within the system then the file wouldn't necessarily open up on the screen like that. Finally, when Willow is scanning the pages, she's only got the scanner on part of them, yet all the text somehow gets scanned in.

This episode broached a very important topic — potential danger on the Internet. Many people use the Internet as their primary form of communication, which means the amount of information being passed around on a daily basis is overwhelming. Of all the horrors and demons represented on the show, this is one of the most realistic.

Whedon must have anticipated how big the *Buffy* Internet phenomenon would become — this exploration of how dangerous it can be is very relevant today. As Buffy, Ms. Calendar, and Giles speculate on what could happen if someone had access to the world's computers, the possibilities are mind-boggling: private letters could be made public; bank accounts altered; hospital records erased; nuclear systems set off. "I Robot, You Jane" is our introduction to Ms. Calendar, who was not originally intended to be a recurring character. The banter between her and Giles showed a spark of chemistry and the writers decided to go with it. The arguments between the two, however, are very black and white — either you surf the Net or you read books — and don't allow the possibility of the two worlds ever successfully overlapping.

"I Robot, You Jane" had a lot of potential, but the result is my least favorite episode of Season One.

HIGHLIGHT: The gang realizing they'll never be able to date normal people as long as they remain on the hellmouth.

NITPICKS: Alyson Hannigan mentioned in an interview that she felt strange talking to her computer while typing. Why didn't they just show us the screen while she typed? It worked on *Doogie Howser*.

OOPS: Now, this is an error that is so obvious it must have been an inside joke. When Moloch finds Buffy's records on the principal's computer, it says she's a sophomore born 10/24/80. However, when he transfers the files to Fritz's computer, it reads she's a senior, born 05/06/79. (Both agree that her GPA is 2.8.) Perhaps this inconsistency is an allusion to the fact that Kristy Swanson's movie Buffy is a senior, while the television Buffy is a sophomore. Also, if you watch the scene frame by frame where Moloch is flipping through various records, you'll see the same five or six faces flash by in a loop.

BEST POP CULTURE REFERENCE: Buffy explaining to Giles that she knows something is wrong: "My spider sense is tingling," a reference to the cartoon *Spiderman*. Whenever Spiderman's spidey sense would start tingling, he knew something was about to happen.

1.9 The Puppet Show

ORIGINAL AIR DATE: May 5, 1997
WRITTEN BY: Dean Batali and Rob Des Hotel
DIRECTED BY: Ellen S. Pressman

GUEST CAST: Kristine Sutherland as Joyce Summers
Richard Werner as Morgan
Burke Roberts as Marc
Armin Shimerman as Principal Snyder
Lenora May as Mrs. Jackson
Chasen Hampton as Elliot
Natasha Pearce as Lisa
Tom Wyner as Sid's voice

When students are found dead with organs missing, the gang suspects a ventriloquist's dummy that appears to have come to life.

This may be the funniest episode in the first season. Sid, the wisecracking dummy, is absolutely hilarious. The setting is the annual school "talentless" show, where magicians can't perform their tricks, actors can't act, and Cordelia sings a wretched version of "The Greatest Love of All." It also features our introduction to Principal Snyder — or, as Giles calls him, "Our new Führer" — played by Armin Shimerman, who is best known as the Ferengi Quark on *Deep Space Nine*. He introduces himself with one of the funniest lines on the show yet, made funnier because of his seriousness: "My predecessor may have gone in for all that touchy-feely relating nonsense, but he was eaten." In "The Pack," the gang had discussed how the school would find a new principal and concluded the only way that one would come in is if he hadn't been told what happened. So the fact that Snyder accepted the job knowing what happened to Flutie immediately casts suspicion on him, reinforced by hints that he might be the demon the gang is searching for.

The ventriloquist's dummy is very eerie, and the speed with which he runs around Buffy's room is terrifying! (Sarah Michelle Gellar admitted to having nightmares about puppets after filming this episode.) The voice for Sid was perfect, as it captured the essence of a tough-talking, cigar-chomping gangster-type from the 1930s. Sid's deep voice is also unexpected, as we often think of dummies having high-pitched voices. One item that is left unexplained is why Morgan was chosen as the person who would own Sid. Why was Sid so cruel to him? Sid mentions that before he had been cursed into the dummy's body, he'd had a fling with a Korean slayer; this tell us that slayers are international, not just from the US.

Once again, as she did in "Teacher's Pet" when Dr. Gregory died, Cordelia goes into a melodramatic, self-absorbed mourning process for the dancer who is killed. We soon discover — unsurprisingly — that her biggest fear was that she could have been the victim. However, where Cordelia was hurtful to Willow in the pilot and downright vicious to Amy in "The Witch," she seems to have toned down to a self-obsessed comic device, and has become far more likable. In the second season she'll deliver some of the funniest lines.

This episode is the first and only time the show continued during the credits. The gang's pathetic attempt at Greek tragedy is hysterical, as are the looks from the members of the audience. This great episode swayed away from vampires entirely, but contained some of the best lines yet.

HIGHLIGHT: Xander playing with the dummy and doing his own act with it in the library.

NITPICKS: Joyce comes in to Buffy's room and says she noticed something seems to be bothering her. A girl was just killed at school — what does she expect?

INTERESTING FACT: When Buffy is looking for Morgan and she walks under the stage, look at the wall behind her — there's a picture of Moloch.

BEST POP CULTURE REFERENCE: After Sid tells the gang he's on their side and then disappears, Xander asks, "Does anybody else feel like they've been Kaiser Soze'd?" To understand that reference, you must see the brilliant 1992 film, *The Usual Suspects*. To explain Xander's reference would spoil the movie, so just trust me and go rent it.

1.10 Nightmares

ORIGINAL AIR DATE: May 12, 1997
TELEPLAY BY: David Greenwalt
STORY BY: Joss Whedon
DIRECTED BY: Bruce Seth Green

GUEST CAST: Andrew J. Ferchland as The Anointed One
Dean Butler as Hank Summers
Jeremy Foley as Billy Palmer
Justin Urich as Wendel
J. Robin Miller as Laura
Terry Cain as Ms. Tishler
Scott Harlan as Aldo Gianfranco
Brian Pietro as Coach

All of the worst nightmares of the people of Sunnydale begin coming true, and Buffy and the gang must find out what is causing this before the world is destroyed.

What's your worst nightmare? In most television shows or movies it's getting caught in a burning building, falling off a cliff, boat, or roller-coaster, or some other disaster. But what about having your father tell you that you were a mistake?

"Nightmares" is eerie simply because Whedon has his finger on the pulse of teenage life. He knows what worries teens, what scares them, what makes them happy. So in this episode, their nightmares are extensions of their own personalities. Cordelia fears having a bad-hair day, wearing nerdy clothing, and being dragged into the chess club. Xander — the clown of the gang — ironically has a dire fear of clowns. Giles suddenly gets lost in his beloved stacks and can't read. Willow is faced with a crowd of people who expect her to do what she cannot. All of these phobias may not sound like appropriate devices for a horror film, but that's because they're far more realistic fears.

The worst of the nightmares is when Buffy's father shows up to tell her that he and her mother separated because of her. This would be devastating to any child of a divorce, and considering how many kids tend to believe all family catastrophes really are their fault, to actually hear one's parent tell them that in the cruel way Hank Summers does would be heartbreaking. During this scene, Buffy's face moves from a look of shock to being utterly crushed by the most important man in her life. Even after she realizes it's not real, the experience itself will probably leave a scar that won't heal right away.

Ironically, the only one who has the courage to fight against his demons is Xander. Only when he decides to stop running is he able to destroy the fear of a clown that has dogged him all his life. It's not clear why Billy's out-of-body experience is affecting everyone else, although things don't need explanations when you live on a hellmouth. His nightmare — an abusive coach who looks like a deformed monster — is something that many boys experience, but their parents don't realize the seriousness of the situation.

While it's understandable that the residents of Sunnydale rationalize the other weird occurrences on the hellmouth, it's hard to believe that all the biblical disasters that befall them could so easily be forgotten. Near the end the nightmares get worse, and Giles faces his worst nightmare, Buffy's death, while Buffy faces hers — becoming a vampire. The scene where Giles kneels before Buffy's grave is a poignant one, for we realize how much he cares about her.

"Nightmares" was spooky, but the saddest part about it was the fact that Buffy's nightmares outnumber everyone else's. It would seem that her problems with being a slayer and a teenager aren't limited to haunting her waking hours. The hellmouth might produce a lot of scary demons, but nothing is as terrifying as our own imaginations.

HIGHLIGHT: The "Smoking Kills" poster on the wall in the basement and the dramatic irony it creates.

NITPICKS: At the end, Xander admits he was still attracted to Buffy when she was a vampire. So why can't he understand her attraction to Angel? Also, the audience boos Willow when she tries to sing, but the male opera singer is pretty lame, too. And how does Buffy retain her soul when *she* becomes a vampire (and somehow get to the hospital during the day)?

OOPS: In "I Robot, You Jane," as mentioned, we find out Buffy was born either in 1979 or 1980, yet in this episode her tombstone reads, "1981–1997." What gives?

INTERESTING FACT: Dean Butler, who plays Buffy's father (and went uncredited in this episode), is best known as Almanzo Wilder on *Little House on the Prairie*.

BEST POP CULTURE REFERENCE: When Billy wakes up he echoes Judy Garland at the end of *The Wizard of Oz* (1939): "I had the strangest dream. . . . And you were there, and you were there. . . ."

1.11 Invisible Girl

ORIGINAL AIR DATE: May 19, 1997
TELEPLAY BY: Ashley Gable and Thomas A. Swyden
STORY BY: Joss Whedon
DIRECTED BY: Reza Badiyi

GUEST CAST: Clea DuVall as Marcie Ross
Ryan Bittle as Mitch
Denise Y. Dowse as Ms. Miller
Julie Fulton as FBI Teacher
John Knight as Bud 1
Mercedes McNab as Harmony
Skip Stellrecht as Agent Manetti
Marc Phelan as Agent Doyle

When an invisible person starts attacking students, Buffy and the gang must try to figure out who it is so they can stop her.

Although "Invisible Girl" tended to meander in spots, it contained the best ending yet. As with "The Pack," this is an episode about popularity and what lack of acceptance can do to a person. As usual, the plight of an outside person mirrors someone in the gang, and in this case it's Buffy. Just as Marcie became invisible because the students and teachers treated her that way, Buffy often feels like an outsider. Xander and Willow share a joke that she doesn't understand and Cordelia treats her as if she's a complete loser. Buffy, who seems so quick-witted all the time, can't think of a single comeback when faced with an army of popular girls.

Cordelia is her normal "I-am-the-center-of-the-universe" self in this one, although for the first time she shows a hint of humanity, telling Buffy she feels just as alone as the unpopular kids. What is most shocking is the sincerity she exhibits, foreshadowing her character development in Season Two (although a lot of her earnestness has to do with the fact that she's speaking on her favorite topic — herself). Willow and Xander seem to shed the most light on what it's like to be unpopular. They immediately recognize the "Have a nice summer" inscriptions in Marcie's yearbook as the "kiss of death," which is a bit of a hyperbole, but contains truth. Their high school is more realistic than that of other television shows because there aren't just popular kids and unpopular kids but a hierarchy of popularity. Cordy and her friends are at the top, then Buffy and her friends, with various levels descending from there.

Angel appears again, as he did in "Teacher's Pet," for vampire-related reasons, rather than to enlighten Buffy on the immediate situation. He tells Giles he can obtain the Codex, a work that has been lost for centuries, although we never discover how he gets it (the Codex will play a more important role in "Prophecy Girl"). The disturbing thing Giles says about the Codex is that it contains the most complete prophecy of the slayer in the last days. What does he mean by the "last days"? The slayer's last days? The world's last days? Unfortunately, the phrase goes unexplained.

Fittingly, this is the episode where we see that Angel casts no reflection in the mirror, although there is an inconsistency with this use of the mirror and the explanation for it in vampire fiction. In the fiction, a vampire casts no reflection because he has no soul. So shouldn't we be able to see Angel?

The least convincing aspect of this episode is that no one in the gang knows how to interpret Marcie's messages. "Look" and "Listen" are almost always followed by "Learn" — it's a common saying in many schools. Even when they know how Marcie became invisible, they still can't figure out what she means by Look and Listen. Considering that Marcie was a student who once tried reaching out to others, why do they dismiss her as being insane and not try to reach out to her?

The scene with Cordelia was anticlimactic and unbelievable — first of all, Marcie would probably have started slashing at Cordy's face pretty quickly, rather than standing there holding the scalpel long enough for Buffy to escape. Secondly, when Buffy tries to "sense" Marcie's presence, she takes a long time doing so. With

Buffy standing with her eyes closed and her back to Marcie, Marcie definitely had the upper hand and didn't take advantage of it.

However, the very end offers a clever and very funny conspiracy theory. The idea that those FBI assassins who are never caught are actually invisible people who were unpopular in high school is hilarious. Overall, an entertaining episode.

HIGHLIGHT: Cordelia's never-ending May Queen acceptance speech: "Ask not what your country can do for you; ask, 'Hey, what am I going to wear to the Spring Fling?' "

NITPICKS: Considering that Cordy tends to repress her memories of bad events, how does she know to come to Buffy for help? Also, she says that it's her first time in the library, yet she was the one who directed Buffy there in the first episode.

OOPS: While Cordelia is giving her May Queen speech, notice how Principal Snyder appears and disappears behind her.

BEST POP CULTURE REFERENCE: The concept of this episode was borrowed from the 1933 film *The Invisible Man*, and the many sequels that followed it.

INTERESTING FACT: The original title of this episode was "Out of Mind, Out of Sight."

1.12 Prophecy Girl

ORIGINAL AIR DATE: June 2, 1997
WRITTEN BY: Joss Whedon
DIRECTED BY: Joss Whedon

GUEST CAST: Kristine Sutherland as Joyce Summers
               Mark Metcalf as The Master
               Robia LaMorte as Jenny Calendar
               Andrew J. Ferchland as The Anointed One
               Scott Gurney as Kevin

Giles reads the prophecy that Buffy will die by the Master's hand, and at 16 years old she is faced with the reality of her own death.

Whew! This was a fast-paced, well acted, emotionally charged episode that brought the entire first season to a brilliant conclusion. If the ending of this felt like closure, it should: faced with the possibility of *Buffy the Vampire Slayer* not being renewed for a second season, Whedon had to reassure the fans that the gang would be all right. Ms. Calendar is back, foreshadowing her return as a major character in the second season. She and Giles exhibit more of the chemistry that was apparent in "I Robot, You Jane." She becomes the latest member of the "club," as Willow refers to it — if this keeps up, there will be fewer people in Sunnydale who *don't* know about the slayer than those who do!

The best part of this episode is how the characters must try to come to terms with death. We all must die someday, but it's only when we are given a date that death assumes a horrific reality. Otherwise people tend not to spend every day thinking how they are getting closer to death with each passing minute. The same goes for Buffy: despite her job's extreme danger, she's never fully realized that there's a very real possibility she could die while carrying out her duty. Her reality is best summed up when she tells Giles, "I have to meet my terrible fate — biology." To a high school student, *classes* should be the most horrific thing in their lives, not the concept of their own mortality. However, when she overhears Giles relating the prophecy to Angel, she reacts at first with laughter, then disbelief, and finally denial, refusing to fulfill her duty as the slayer. She has her whole life ahead of her, and Sarah is wonderful in this scene, reminding us not to forget that a slayer is still human.

Willow, too, is jolted into reality when her fellow students from the AV club are murdered. Until now she has reacted with disgust and disbelief to the strange occurrences around her, but so far none of the victims have been close to her. This loss is very real, however, and she'll be reminded of it each time she enters the AV room alone. Alyson puts in her best performance yet as the traumatized victim, crying to Buffy about how cruel and unfair life is. It is Willow's reaction to these grisly deaths that seems to spur Buffy on to face the Master.

The scene with Buffy and her mother is one of the few times they seem to connect. When Joyce shows her the dress, Buffy seems genuinely appreciative, whereas up to this point one or the other of them has always pulled away. Joyce tells the story of how she met Hank with no resentment, demonstrating that she seems to have gotten past the divorce.

Xander decides to take his crush on Buffy one step further, with devastating consequences. Unlike many similar rejections on television, we've watched Xander pine for Buffy all season, and we understand the pain he's feeling. Turning him down must have been one of the most difficult things Buffy has had to do, and Willow's anxiety while waiting to hear the result must have been nerve-racking. A cheer should go out for Willow, though, for having the courage to also turn Xander down, knowing his proposal to her wasn't heartfelt. Poor Xander.

This episode was rated TV14, most likely for the gory exit of the Master. Buffy's death at the time was a shock, for, without knowing if the show was to be renewed for a second season, one might have thought there was a possibility (albeit a tiny one) that it would end that way. Buffy's state of paralysis when the Master stands behind her is an extension of her previous fear of death. As a single tear rolls down her terrified face, this is Sarah's best performance yet. Angel's inability to perform CPR is the first mention we get that a vampire has no breath, but one that will lead to inconsistencies in the second season. The scene on the rooftop between Buffy and the Master is the funniest dialogue of the season, partly because Buffy is still shaken and the Master doesn't exactly understand what she's talking about.

The creature from the hellmouth was an amazing effect, although Giles kept referring to it as the hellmouth itself. Is the hellmouth concrete? A monster? In literature it is the portal between Earth and Hell, the passageway through which one can move from one existence to another. Many Renaissance morality plays made mention of a hellmouth, and it is believed by some that when Jesus was crucified he traveled through the hellmouth to carry the souls of the just — such as Noah, Adam, and Eve — to Heaven, where they rightfully belonged.

"Prophecy Girl" was a superb episode, featuring standout performances by all involved. Despite Whedon wrapping the story up so well, it's possible there would have been a revolt against the network if the series hadn't been renewed — a television show this good demands continuation.

HIGHLIGHT: The rooftop banter between Buffy and the Master.

NITPICKS: Buffy charging toward the library with her theme music playing has got to be the single cheesiest moment on *Buffy* ever. Also, Buffy says to Joyce that they can't afford the white dress. Who buys Buffy's clothes? They aren't exactly Wal-Mart brands, and considering Buffy doesn't have a paying job, Joyce must be paying for that designer wardrobe.

OOPS: If there's a skylight over the library, why has the only sunlight we've ever seen there come from the side windows? There is never a beam coming from directly overhead. Also, when Cordelia is talking to Ms. Calendar in the car, her mouth isn't moving. And at the end, when Buffy is facedown in the water, notice how her hair goes from being piled up on top of her head to being loose and around her shoulders.

BEST POP CULTURE REFERENCE: Xander says, "Calm may work for Locutus of the Borg here, but I'm freaked out and I intend to stay that way!" In *Star Trek: The Next Generation*, the crew came across a race of beings that existed as a collective, referring to themselves only as part of a group. These beings, The Borg, showed no emotions, and in one episode Jean-Luc Picard was assimilated into the race. His name was Locutus of Borg.

SEASON TWO
(SEPTEMBER 1997–MAY 1998)

2.1 When She Was Bad

ORIGINAL AIR DATE: September 15, 1997
WRITTEN BY: Joss Whedon
DIRECTED BY: Joss Whedon

GUEST CAST: Dean Butler as Hank Summers
Kristine Sutherland as Joyce Summers
Robia LaMorte as Ms. Calendar
Andrew J. Ferchland as The Anointed One
Armin Shimerman as Principal Snyder
Brent Jennings as Absalom
Tamara Braun as Tara

After being away in LA for the summer, Buffy returns to Sunnydale a very different person.

While "Prophecy Girl" ended on a relieved, upbeat note, "When She Was Bad" involves a lot of people getting hurt, mostly by Buffy. When Buffy makes her action-packed entrance, she seems normal, although perhaps a little distant. (When you haven't seen your friends for an entire summer, you might be a little withdrawn from them at first.) Once Willow and Xander mention the Master, though, gloom shrouds Buffy's face. Why does she act the way she does? Has she associated her hatred of vampires with the people who live there and thus can't separate her feelings for one from those for the other? Has she gone into a depression and only snaps out of it when she takes a sledgehammer to the Master's bones? Regardless of her personal problems — which, admittedly, are immense — what she does to those around her is beyond insensitive, casting a suspicious light on how Buffy treats her friends.

Given that, it's ironic that Cordelia of all people should be the one to give her the pep talk. Isn't her stance hypocritical? Where does she get off calling Buffy the bitch of the year? The main difference between Buffy and Cordelia in this episode is that Buffy manipulates those who are her friends and intends to hurt them as badly as she can, whereas Cordy tends to pick on those who aren't her friends, and her insults drop people a notch or two without destroying them. In this episode Buffy hurts everyone around her, Angel worries that he may have hurt her, and Xander unknowingly hurts Willow by seeming to forget entirely that they nearly locked lips at the beginning of the episode. Speaking of the kiss that almost happened, shouldn't that have had a greater effect on Willow and Xander? Does he really forget about it or just pretend to? It's difficult to tell whether they would actually have kissed, for they pull away from one another just before the vampire pops up. However, Xander's threat to Buffy — "If anything happens to Willow, I'll kill you" — proves that while his infatuations lie elsewhere, Willow is the one he truly cares about. Notice how he holds her after releasing her from the chains.

The fight scene at the end was great. In other action shows, like *Xena* or *Highlander*, the enemies tend to take on the hero one by one, rather than attacking en masse. In this episode vampires attack Buffy in twos or threes, and she still holds her own. When she destroys the bones of the Master, she destroys the demons within her that have plagued her for months and she's ready to move on.

"When She Was Bad" was a good season premiere, but I find it hard to believe that Buffy could have acted that way. It was a little disappointing to come back to the show like this.

HIGHLIGHT: The creepy dream Buffy has where Giles turns into the Master.

NITPICKS: Was it just me or did parts of this show seem like a glorified ad for Cibo Matto? And why didn't Giles simply burn the Master's bones rather than bury them?

OOPS: When Willow, Cordy, Jenny, and Giles are rolled out hanging upside-down, Giles's hand brushes the Master's rib cage and you can see it move, as if it were made of rubber. Also, after Buffy stakes the first vampire, the camera is positioned over the skeleton for us to watch the fight, but the four are no longer hanging there. And Buffy breaks the Master's rib cage on the second blow with the sledgehammer, but when Angel walks around behind her, the rib cage is intact.

INTERESTING FACT: The credits for the second season included David Boreanaz for the first time, and where the "In every generation . . ." speech had been read by the WB announcer for the first season, it is now recited by Anthony Stewart Head.

MUSIC/BANDS: As Angel leaves Buffy's room, the song playing is "It Doesn't Matter" by Allison Krauss and Union Station, from the CD *So Long So Wrong.* The song continues as Joyce drives Buffy to school. As Willow and Xander wait for Buffy to arrive at The Bronze, the band on stage is Cibo Matto (with Sean Lennon on bass guitar) and the song is "Spoon," from the CD *Super Relax.* Buffy does her sexy dance with Xander to "Sugar Water," from Cibo Matto's CD *Vive! La Woman.* The score for this episode was written by Christophe Beck.

BEST POP CULTURE REFERENCE: Cordelia says, "Whatever is causing the Joan Collins 'tude, deal with it." Joan Collins played the mega-bitch, Alexis, on *Dynasty* for eight years.

2.2 Some Assembly Required

ORIGINAL AIR DATE: September 22, 1997
WRITTEN BY: Ty King
DIRECTED BY: Bruce Seth Green

GUEST CAST: Angelo Spizzirri as Eric
Ingo Neuhaus as Daryl Epps
Michael Bacall as Chris
Robin LaMorte as Ms. Calendar
Melanie MacQueen as Mrs. Epps
Amanda Wilmshurst as Cheerleader

A Dr. Frankenstein wannabe tries to reconstruct a woman after restoring his brother to life, but to obtain a head he must kill a living girl — Cordelia.

"Some Assembly Required" was creepy beyond words, and too
obviously a takeoff of *Frankenstein* to be taken seriously. If the
revivification of one's brother was supposed to be a metaphor for
some high school problem, then its symbolism wasn't too clear. The
basic plot is borrowed heavily from Mary Shelley's *Frankenstein*,
where a scientist reconstructs a body from parts of corpses to try
to create life. Science has often tried tampering with Nature, but
when Dr. Frankenstein attempts to recreate the birth process, his
efforts are met with terrifying results. He shuns the creature, who
must go out alone and try to learn about the world around him.
Eventually, after being spurned by a family he'd grown to love, the
creature returns to Frankenstein and demands that he make a
woman. Frankenstein reluctantly obliges, but before the process is
over he realizes he cannot commit the same mistake he made before,
and he destroys her, causing the creature to go on a murderous rampage.

In "Some Assembly Required," the story is similar, although it's
used as a backdrop to an episode about relationships. Giles agonizes
over whether or not he should ask out Ms. Calendar, Buffy and
Angel's relationship sparks up again, and Willow and Xander complain that they always end up alone. When Xander rescues Cordelia,
however, we see the first hint that she's attracted to him, although
he misses it completely. There's also a certain sadness to the episode
— where Buffy faces her own mortality in "Prophecy Girl," Chris
has had to deal with his brother's death and his mother's subsequent
depression. Chris — and everyone else, for that matter — becomes
as invisible to his mother as Marcie was to everyone in "Invisible
Girl." Chris Epps is arguably the smartest student in school, but in
high school it is the sports figures who really matter, and Chris
can never live up to his brother's reputation as an all-star running
back. In other words, some assembly is required in all of these
relationships.

Cordelia acts like the stereotypical horror-movie scream queen.
Despite several warnings, she still takes no precautions. After hear-
ing that female corpses have gone missing, she walks across a dark
parking lot alone. Then she stays behind in the change room to apply
her makeup, almost getting kidnapped. And after escaping *that*, she
walks behind the bleachers alone to get a drink. Wake up, Cordy!

This episode was important to the development of everyone's
relationships, but other than that it was a gratuitous use of the
Frankenstein story without adding anything to it.

HIGHLIGHT: Xander playing with the plastic head in science class.

NITPICKS: The photos that Eric flips through don't match up with the poses the characters were in when he took them earlier. In Eric's shots, they all appear to be posing for him, yet earlier they were holding up hands and getting caught off guard.

MUSIC/BANDS: Score by Christophe Beck, with Adam Fields.

BEST POP CULTURE REFERENCE: Buffy tries to hint to Willow that she's needed in the library for some computer hacking: "Sorry to interrupt, Willow, but . . . bat signal." The bat signal was a glowing image of a bat that the mayor of Gotham City shined into the sky to summon Batman when he was needed.

2.3 School Hard

ORIGINAL AIR DATE: September 29, 1997
TELEPLAY BY: David Greenwalt
STORY BY: David Greenwalt and Joss Whedon
DIRECTED BY: John T. Kretchmer

GUEST CAST: Kristine Sutherland as Joyce Summers
Robia LaMorte as Ms. Calendar
Andrew J. Ferchland as The Anointed One
Brian Reddy as Police Chief Bob
James Marsters as Spike
Juliet Landau as Drusilla
Armin Shimerman as Principal Snyder
Alexandra Johnes as Sheila

Sunnydale's newest vampire residents, Spike and Drusilla, arrive in town just in time for Parent–Teacher Night at Sunnydale High.

Spike and Drusilla are without a doubt the two coolest and creepiest characters on television. This co-dependent couple will wreak havoc on Sunnydale for the rest of the season, yet they'll have viewers begging for more. Spike is a Billy Idol lookalike, a British rebel vampire who has arrived from Prague with Drusilla, the mentally disturbed, childlike, weak vampire who depends on Spike for survival. Immediately there is something different about these two, a sense that perhaps Spike, too, has retained his soul but not a conscience. Why else would he care so deeply for Drusilla? When he makes his first appearance before the Anointed he talks tough and nasty, informing him he's killed two slayers and he'll kill another. When Dru enters, his face changes back to normal — a special effect we haven't seen since Darla's face transformed in the

EVERETT COLLECTION/WARNER BROS.

pilot episode — and he talks in a cuddlier voice to her. Notice Spike always tends to keep his game face off when he's with Dru.

As if the arrival of these two didn't cause enough problems for Buffy, Snyder is riding her again, telling her he's looking for any reason to expel her. Why is she sitting in the office with a girl who stabbed her teacher with pruning shears when the only offense he charges Buffy with is burning down the gym of her last school? First of all, that's an offense she's already atoned for, and secondly, why doesn't he instead attribute the destruction of the library to her? They never did explain who got blamed for that. However, this is an important episode in shaping your attitude toward Principal Snyder —it's hinted for the first time that he knows more about what's going on than we think. His standard response for strange occurrences is that it's PCP/gang-related, and that explanation keeps coming up a little too readily for comfort. At the end we're led to believe that the police are covering up the hellmouth activity as well.

The relationship between Buffy and Joyce is precarious once again, but Joyce's character is inconsistent in this episode. First she tells Buffy that she doesn't want to be disappointed in her again, when Buffy hasn't done anything wrong. What kind of incentive is her mother offering her when she clearly doesn't trust her to do anything right? At Parent–Teacher Night, when the vampires jump through the window Joyce just stands there, exhibiting absolutely no look of surprise, leading some members of the *Buffy* mailing lists to speculate that Joyce was once a slayer herself. After looking infuriated with Buffy immediately before the vampires enter, she allows Buffy to tell her what to do and doesn't drag Buffy into the locked classroom afterward, almost as if she knows that Buffy can handle the gang. For all of her pride and acceptance of Buffy at the end, she will soon forget and go back to badgering her daughter in subsequent episodes the way she used to.

We discover that Spike — a.k.a. William the Bloody — was actually turned into a vampire by Angel, which probably adds to Angel's enormous sense of guilt about his past. Not only is Angel responsible for the people he has killed, but for the people who die at the hands of those whom he has turned into vampires. The chain reaction Angel has caused is infinite. When Angel is first reunited with Spike, we get a glimpse of him as the evil Angelus, whom we will meet in all his horrific glory later in the season. He admits to almost sacrificing Xander to Spike, and yet people question why Xander hates Angel so much?

In the end, Spike blames his failure to kill Buffy on her family and friends. To this point in the series Buffy has been told again and again that these outsiders are a hindrance to her, not a help, so it was comforting to know she's doing the right thing by getting her friends involved. Spike's annihilation of the "Annoying One" is a relief, changing the ritualistic traditions of the vampire lair to an each-vampire-for-himself attitude. Spike's rebellion is a refreshing change among the vampires, and fans everywhere applauded his and Dru's arrival. A terrific episode!

HIGHLIGHT: Willow's reaction to Buffy's lemonade.

NITPICKS: Hasn't Giles learned by now that school is important to Buffy? As Buffy is on the verge of being expelled, Giles urges her to cut class and not attend the Parent–Teacher Night. Also, why has Cordelia started hanging out with the gang? A debt of gratitude?

OOPS: How can Spike exhale cigarette smoke if a vampire has no breath?

INTERESTING FACT: Joss Whedon refers to Spike and Dru as the Sid and Nancy of the vampire world. Sid Vicious was the bassist in the punk rock band the Sex Pistols. He died of a heroin overdose while he was about to be tried for the murder of his girlfriend, Nancy Spungen, in 1979.

MUSIC/BANDS: When Willow is helping Buffy study French at The Bronze and Xander is dancing alone, the song playing is "1000 Nights," performed by Nickel. As the three of them hit the dance floor, "Stupid Thing" comes on. Both are from Nickel's album, *Stupid Thing*. Score by Shawn Clement and Sean Murray.

BEST POP CULTURE REFERENCE: Spike to Angel: "You were my sire, man! You were my Yoda!" Yoda, for all those who live under rocks, was the Jedi Master who trained Luke Skywalker to be a Jedi Knight in *The Empire Strikes Back* (1980).

2.4 Inca Mummy Girl

ORIGINAL AIR DATE: October 6, 1997
WRITTEN BY: Matt Kiene and Joe Reinkemeyer
DIRECTED BY: Ellen S. Pressman

GUEST CAST: Kristine Sutherland as Joyce Summers
Seth Green as Oz
Ara Celi as Ampata

Jason Hall as Devon
Henrik Rosvall as Sven
Joey Crawford as Rodney
Danny Strong as Jonathan
Kristen Winnicki as Gwen
Gil Birmingham as Peru Guy
Samuel Jacobs as Peruvian boy

Xander falls in love with a foreign exchange student who — surprise, surprise — turns out to be an ancient Inca mummy come to life.

This episode draws heavily from the history of the Incas and their practise of mummification. The Inca people were an immensely wealthy nation who prospered until the mid-sixteenth century. The imperial capital was Cuzco (modern-day Peru) and the Incas ruled over Chile, upper Argentina, Ecuador, Peru, Bolivia, and south Columbia — a larger area than any current Andean nation. At its peak, the Inca nation consisted of 12,000,000 people, but only 40,000 of them were actually Inca, ruling like royalty over the others. It was partly the wealth of the nation that led to its downfall. Houses and other buildings were inlaid with silver and gold, and the nation's material wealth was one of the first things explorers recognized during the 1532 Spanish conquest. The Inca emperor was kidnapped and ransomed for a large sum of money, equivalent to about $50 million by today's standards. However, it was mostly smallpox that destroyed the Inca people, killing about two thirds of the population upon contact with the explorers.

The Incas left no written records, and there is much debate about the nature of their religion. They worshipped nature gods, mostly sun and moon. In one of the only written accounts from the time, the Spaniard Father Bernake Cobo described the Inca practice of human sacrifice, which was rare and usually limited to children 10 and under. Occasionally, according to Father Cobo, they would sacrifice a maiden of 15 or 16 years, who had been raised in a convent to prevent any blemishes on her person. The sacrifice would involve her throat being slit or her being hanged, and sometimes the heart was removed while it was still beating. However, considering the author of this account was a Spaniard who probably had to convince his people that the conquest was a *good* thing, we must take his words with a generous dose of wariness.

The Incas were one of many ancient cultures who practised mummification. The mummy as a horror device originated in film, unlike vampires and werewolves, which began as folklore. The original movie, *The Mummy* (1932), starred that incredible monster-movie actor, Boris Karloff, and is about a mummified princess and an Egyptian who tries to restore her to life. One aspect of all mummy stories is reincarnation — either the mummy or someone who loved the mummified person is reincarnated in another life.

In "Inca Mummy Girl," the mummy is a princess who was sacrificed to a mountain god. This mummy was based on a real-life Inca female mummy discovered in 1995. The mummy was completely frozen, which had helped preserve the body. She was found on Mount Ampato in Peru, hence the name, Ampata, in this episode. Ampata is restored to life because of her overwhelming desire to have had a normal life centuries ago.

Once again, the plight of the "demon" mirrors Buffy's own life. When Ampata was a princess she sacrificed her life, love, and her future for her culture. Buffy, too, has given up having a normal life, realizes she might not have a future, and will later sacrifice her love to save the world. The obvious connection is made when Ampata's guard refers to her as the Chosen One. After Ampata is destroyed, Buffy feels sorry for her, finally recognizing how similar they are: Ampata hides a corpse in her trunk, while Buffy hides holy water and stakes in her drawers.

This was another episode about relationships — poor Xander once again falls for a monster, and he is so comfortable around Ampata. Willow becomes depressed when she sees them together, not knowing that Oz has noticed her, and Cordy once again continues her superficial relationship with yet another good-looking guy for whom she couldn't care less. Her treatment of Sven, telling him to get a "fruity drinky" and ordering him around like a dog, is hilarious. When Willow dresses as an Eskimo — complete with harpoon — we realize it isn't her personality and looks that hinder her from a relationship, but the fact that she doesn't let the true Willow come out (see also "Halloween"). Ironically, it's when she's snug in her parka that Oz first notices her.

HIGHLIGHT: Xander showing Ampata how to eat Twinkies.

NITPICKS: Ampata locked lips with Xander for longer than the others — why didn't he turn into a mummy? And could Joyce maybe, just once, act like she's proud of her daughter? The way she gushes over how beautiful Ampata looks while snubbing her own daughter was downright annoying.

OOPS: At the end, when Ampata is choking Xander, from the front her face has turned into the mummy, but from the back she has her long shiny hair and from the side she hasn't become a mummy.

MUSIC/BANDS: During the costume dance at The Bronze, the song is "Shadows" by Four Star Mary, and Xander and Ampata hit the dance floor to "Fate." Both are on Four Star Mary's self-titled CD. (Four Star Mary does the music for Dingoes Ate My Baby whenever they appear on the show.) Score by Christophe Beck.

BEST POP CULTURE REFERENCE: Oz's band is called Dingoes Ate My Baby, a reference to an Australian baby-murder case in which a woman named Lindy Chamberlain claimed a dingo had taken her baby from its crib. Her story kept changing until even her family started to disbelieve her, and she was charged with murder (and eventually acquitted). The 1988 movie *A Cry in the Dark*, starring Meryl Streep and Sam Neill, was based on her story.

2.5 Reptile Boy

ORIGINAL AIR DATE: October 13, 1997
WRITTEN BY: David Greenwalt
DIRECTED BY: David Greenwalt

GUEST CAST: Todd Babcock as Tom Warner
Greg Vaughn as Richard
Todd Babcock as Tom
Jordana Spiro as Callie
Robin Atkin Downes as Machida
Danny Strong as Jonathan
Christopher Dalhberg as Tackle
Jason Posey as Linebacker
Coby Bell as Young Man

When Cordelia and Buffy attend a frat party, they almost become lunch meat for a slimy creature the fraternity worships.

Although this episode was a little ridiculous, the concept of frat boys worshipping a creature in the basement as an analogy for the realities of fraternities is hilarious. On many university and college campuses, sororities and fraternities have gotten out of hand. Initiation rituals have caused deaths, the members often cling together with a pack mentality (see "The Pack"), and in some circles, if you don't make it into a sorority or fraternity, you're doomed to an unpopular existence. Meetings often involve rituals, chants, and candles, and to an outsider may appear very cult-like. Hence this episode.

Despite Buffy's rebellious behavior, she has always acted responsibly. When both she and Cordy drink underage and date older men, they fall into a vicious trap that threatens to destroy them both. The fraternity brothers pray to their god, Machida, who represents the fraternity itself. When they thank Machida for giving them all their wealth and possessions, the insinuation is that without their fraternity they would be nothing. Machida could also represent their masculinity and appeal to women. Notice that when Xander shows no interest in the "psycho cult," he is emasculated and forced to dance in drag. Machida itself is an obvious phallic symbol, slithering from hidden depths and standing up before the three helpless girls. We never actually see the end of the tail, as if it's connected to the frat house in some way.

Continuing the Willow arc in the subplot, she becomes a stronger character when she stands up and lectures Giles and Angel on how they treat Buffy. For the first time, Giles is forced to recognize that the pressure he's putting on a 16-year-old girl may be too much, and Angel realizes that it's difficult for Buffy to date a vampire — because she's so young, he must be more direct in telling her how he feels about her. When he invites her for a coffee, Buffy takes the upper hand, telling him she'll let him know when she's ready. But it was Willow who put the wheels in motion. This episode had its moments, but was a little too over-the-top.

HIGHLIGHT: Cordy's hilarious parking job and that terrific license plate: "Queen C."

NITPICKS: Cordelia gives Buffy a set of rules to follow while at the party, the first of which is not to wear black. When Buffy shows up in a black dress, why doesn't Cordy say anything?

OOPS: Angel couldn't have entered the frat house if he wasn't invited.

MUSIC/BANDS: As Buffy becomes a wallflower at the frat party, the song is "She" by Louie Says. The song, which plays again at the end of the episode when Angel asks her if she'd like to get a coffee, is from the band's CD *Gravity, Suffering, Love and Fate*. Xander does his girlie dance to "Bring Me On" by Act of Faith, from the band's *Scream* CD. The score for this episode was written by Sean Murray and Shawn Clement, and featured the songs "Devil's Lair" (when Cordy and Buffy arrive at the frat party), "If I Can't Have You" (when they run into Richard at the frat house), "Wolves" (when Richard dances with Cordelia), and "Secrets" (when Cordelia lectures her boyfriend at The Bronze on how to get coffee).

BEST POP CULTURE REFERENCE: This isn't so much a reference as it is a "moment." Buffy, Willow, and Xander watch East Indian movies on their nights off, which has actually become a popular activity among people their age and older. Though most people who watch them don't have the luxury of Willow translating for them.

2.6 Halloween

ORIGINAL AIR DATE: October 27, 1997
WRITTEN BY: Carl Ellsworth
DIRECTED BY: Bruce Seth Green

GUEST CAST: Robin Sachs as Ethan Rayne
Juliet Landau as Drusilla
Armin Shimerman as Principal Snyder
Seth Green as Oz
James Marsters as Spike
Larry Bagby III as Larry
Abigail Gershman as Girl

Chaos threatens to befall Sunnydale on Halloween when people turn into whatever they've dressed as.

A Halloween episode was inevitable sooner or later on *Buffy*, and the result was excellent.

Halloween, or All Hallow's Eve, originated as one of the two great pagan festivals of the year. May Day was a great fertility festival which celebrated the arrival of spring and the promise of great harvest, whereas All Hallow's Eve was the beginning of winter, symbolizing death, cold, and darkness. It was believed that on this night chaos ensued — ghosts of relatives entered houses to be with families, fires were lit, fairies and nymphs created mischief. Yet Halloween was always a celebratory festival, and today exists as a fun event for children.

Ironically, Giles tells Buffy and the gang that Halloween is one of the quietest nights of the year for vampires, and that they tend to stay away. When she dresses as the person she'd like to become — an 18th-century French noblewoman — Buffy plays into the hands of Ethan Rayne, an acquaintance of Giles' whose significance will be explained in "The Dark Age." Willow and Buffy steal Giles' watcher diaries only to discover a picture of the person Angel used to love. Cordelia then delivers a biting comment — "When it comes to dating, I'm the slayer" — and Buffy assumes that in order to earn Angel's love she must become someone else.

Spike earns more of the viewer's respect because of his intelligence when it comes to slaying a slayer. He watches her in alleys, videotapes her and watches each move carefully, and later he'll call on a group of bounty hunters to get rid of her. There's a reason he's killed two slayers — he's vicious and very intelligent.

Ethan calls on Chaos — just as the pagans believed Halloween was a night of chaos — and worships the god Janus. Janus was the Roman god with two faces, one looking forward and the other backward. Janus built a city on a hill, named Janicullum, and ruled it all his life. The period of his rule was a time of prosperity with no war and a surplus of food. It was believed that Janus invented money, and his face is emblazoned on the earliest bronze coins. After he died, his people turned him into a god and worshipped him.

It is said that when Janus was deified he became the guardian of doors, allowing certain people into the city and beating unwelcome people with a stick. His two faces allowed him to watch both directions. Perhaps it is because *Buffy the Vampire Slayer* is about a "doorway" — the hellmouth — that Janus is invoked here. Janus has also been used in modern literature to symbolize hypocrisy and the dual nature of things, or as Giles puts it, the division of self into female and male (anima/animus), good and evil. (Giles has always been more Jungian than Freudian.) In that case, the division of self becomes literal — on the outside, Buffy is tough, but on the inside she wants to be someone with whom Angel will fall in love; Xander must let Buffy fight the battles, but deep down he wishes he could take charge; Willow is extremely shy and lets very few see her wonderful personality, and inside she's an attractive woman (with amazing abs) just waiting to be noticed.

The most surprising part of this episode is our first glimpse of Giles as the Ripper. We'll see more of this behavior with an explanation in "The Dark Age," but suffice it to say it was a shocker watching this "fuddy duddy" suddenly become tough *and* angry. Go, Giles!

"Halloween" was an intriguing episode, well written, with great acting from all.

HIGHLIGHT: Giles' reaction when Willow, who has become a ghost, walks through the wall.

NITPICKS: As funny as it is, Willow walking through walls is unrealistic. Since she doesn't feel any differently, wouldn't she instinctively use the door, as usual?

OOPS: Buffy's house door opens the wrong way in this episode and in "Inca Mummy Girl" — from inside the house, the doorknob should be on the right, not the left. And when Giles tells Willow to leave him and Ethan alone, she turns and brushes a curtain and closes the door. How can she do either of those things if she's a ghost?

MUSIC/BANDS: As Angel waits for Buffy and gets caught up in a conversation with Cordelia, the song playing is "Shy" by Epperley, found on their self-titled album. As Willow crosses the street in front of Oz's van, his stereo is playing "How She Died" by Treble Charger, from their CD *Maybe It's Me*. Score by Christophe Beck.

BEST POP CULTURE REFERENCE: Willow on Buffy's helplessness: "She couldn't have dressed up like Xena?"

2.7 Lie to Me

ORIGINAL AIR DATE: November 3, 1997
WRITTEN BY: Joss Whedon
DIRECTED BY: Joss Whedon

GUEST CAST: Robia LaMorte as Jenny Calendar
James Marsters as Spike
Jason Behr as Billy "Ford" Fordham
Juliet Landau as Drusilla
Jarrad Paul as Diego
Will Rothhaar as James
Julia Lee as Chantarelle
Todd McIntosh as "Hi" Vampire

An old school friend of Buffy's comes to town, but he belongs to a cult of vampire worshippers and wants to become a vampire.

One of the most important issues on *Buffy the Vampire Slayer* is that of trust. Buffy trusts that her friends won't betray her secret, that Giles will be there for her, and that Angel won't bite her. Her friends trust her to save them when they're faced with vampires, and Giles trusts that Buffy won't bail out on her duty. However, that trust has slowly been breaking down over past episodes. In "Reptile Boy," Buffy tells Giles that she and her mother are ill, when she really needs the night off to go to a frat party. In "Halloween," she and Willow steal one of Giles' watcher diaries, while Buffy makes up stories about what Ms. Calendar said about him. Those lies pile up unstoppably in "Lie to Me."

In this episode, almost everyone lies to Buffy. Xander, Willow, and Angel look into Ford's past without telling her; Ford tells Buffy he killed a vampire; Angel tells her he stayed at home when he actually saw Drusilla. Spike also lies to Ford, and Ford subsequently lies to the vampire wannabes. After all that, Angel tells Buffy to trust him that Ford is no good. Can we blame her when she doesn't believe him?

The vampire club was an interesting aspect of this episode, and it's fitting that the writers would make fun of vampire wannabes because in Whedon's mythology vampires are all so vicious. However, occasionally Whedon *does* romanticize his vampires. Spike and Drusilla have a co-dependent relationship and both are attractive, while Angel — a vampire, lest we forget — is the male sex symbol of the series. The writers mock the Anne Rice/gothic mentality, where dressing in black, listening to Bauhaus and holding up Lestat as the ultimate leading man is the norm.

There does exist, however, a vampire subculture that is hidden from the general population. While these self-described "vampires" crave and drink blood, they do not change into bats or live eternally or hunt victims. Vampire clubs have even popped up worldwide, where these people can meet others with similar interests and engage in "vampire activity."

Buffy and Angel continue to play games with one another. After "Halloween" had such an intimate ending between the two, Buffy is once again making Angel jealous while he lies to her. First she dances with Xander to drive him crazy, then she shrugs off his date for a coffee, and now she hangs out with Ford. To her, Angel's lies and mystery cause suspicion, but it's also amusing to see a 242-year-old vampire going through the same mind games and manipulations that an 18-year-old guy would.

When we discover Ford's plight, it is difficult not to feel sorry for him, because in a roundabout way his fate is similar to Buffy's. Buffy complains that it's not fair for a 16-year-old girl to have to think about death, yet so far she's been able to beat it. Ford is dying and knows roughly how long he has left. However, unlike Buffy who, despite *all* her complaining, accepts that she might die and is willing to sacrifice her life to save humanity, Ford refuses to accept his fate and is willing to sacrifice his friends to extend his life.

The most important element of this episode is that we learn how Drusilla became a vampire. Like Ford, her life was sacrificed and she seeks revenge as a result. However, for the first time we realize how vicious Angelus was. He didn't just attack individuals, but also their families and everyone around them. Where other vampires kill because of their need for blood, Angelus had a sadistic desire to watch people suffer. This revelation foreshadows what will happen in "Innocence" and afterward. The writers make Angel's past so vivid that we just know we're eventually going to witness him in action.

"Lie to Me" was an important episode, and its message was made clear at the end: Sometimes telling a lie is much kinder than revealing the truth.

HIGHLIGHT: Ford instructing Spike on how a vampire is supposed to act.

NITPICKS: Ford mentions Angel's hand is cold. Is Angel cold like a corpse? If so, the thought of him and Buffy together in "Surprise" is enough to give any viewer the wiggins. When the vampires are feeding on the wannabes, they feed for a long time — why don't the wannabes turn into vampires? Finally, Ford wasn't registered at Sunnydale, suggesting he came alone, without his family. Why, then, is he buried in Sunnydale?

INTERESTING FACT: The movie that Ford lip-synchs to at the vampire club is the 1973 version of *Dracula*, in which the Count is played by Jack Palance. Also, one of the vampires is played by Todd McIntosh, who is the show's makeup wizard.

MUSIC/BANDS: As Xander, Willow, and Ford play pool at The Bronze, the song playing is "Lois, On The Brink" by Willoughby, from the CD *Be Better Soon*. When Angel, Willow, and Xander visit the vampire club, it's "Never Land" by those goth lords, Sisters of Mercy, from their album *Floodland*. However, this song was only used in the original airing of the episode, and for some reason (copyright, perhaps?) it was removed from later airings. Repeats of the show feature a song scored by Sean Murray and Shawn Clement. As they leave the club, you can hear Creaming Jesus performing "Reptile," from the *Gothic Rock* compilation album.

BEST POP CULTURE REFERENCE: Buffy tells Ford in front of the others, "I moped over you for months. Sitting in my room listening to that Divinyls song 'I Touch Myself.'" She quickly catches herself and explains that she didn't know what the song meant. In the 1991 hit "I Touch Myself," the singer confesses that she touches herself when she thinks about the person she loves. A lot of young people who bought the single likely had no idea what the song was actually about.

ORIGINAL AIR DATE: November 19, 1997
WRITTEN BY: Dean Batali and Rob Des Hotel
DIRECTED BY: Bruce Seth Green

GUEST CAST: Robin Sachs as Ethan Rayne
Robia LaMorte as Jenny Calendar
Stuart McLean as Philip Henry
Wendy Way as Dierdre
Michael Earl Reid as Custodian
Daniel Henry Murray as Creepy Cult Guy
Carlease Burke as Detective Winslow

Giles reveals his past as "Ripper," and a demon that he and his friends conjured up in university comes back to kill him.

Just when you thought Giles was the only adult you could completely trust, along comes a dark past and a strange nickname. This episode was great, if only to see Giles completely lose it for the first time. In a strange twist, throughout this show the roles of Buffy and Giles are switched, and while Giles becomes rebellious, refusing to talk to anyone and caring too much for Jenny to pay attention to anyone else, Buffy becomes practical and authoritative, forcing Giles to talk to her. This state of reversal is established at the beginning of the episode, where we see Giles' dream, not Buffy's, as we are used to. The difference is, Giles lacks Buffy's gift of prophecy because he is a watcher, not a slayer. Instead his dreams look back to a past he'd prefer to forget, although they do signal to him that his past is about to return.

The whole story of Eyghon, the tattoos, and the relapse is intriguing and acts as a metaphor for drug experimentation in high school and university. The experience with Eyghon got out of hand and one person "O.D.'d" on the demon and died. Giles thought if he could quit then he would never have any problems, but he can't hide the marks on his arm. Eventually he has a relapse, separates himself from his friends, and pulls a "lost weekend," as Buffy puts it (a reference to the 1945 film where the main character goes on a weekend bender and separates himself from everyone he knows). After his "relapse" threatens the lives of those around him — even passing the addiction on to one of them — he quits and the demon leaves him forever. It would have made a great Jefferson Airplane song.

Buffy comes through in a way we haven't seen before. Putting everything aside, she refuses to allow Giles to push her away, and it is she who instructs the others on what to do. Notice how Cordy steps up to receive her instructions from Buffy, something she never would have done a few episodes ago.

The special effects in "The Dark Age" were amazing — they have yet to be topped. Robia LaMorte, who plays Jenny, said the Eyghon makeup almost brought on an anxiety attack: "They put this stuff all over your eyes and ears and all you have are two little nose holes to breathe out of. . . . Things start to go through your head, of seeing yourself jumping out of the chair and ripping the thing off" (qtd. in Boris, "*Buffy*"). And the scene where Angel's demon fights Eyghon is superb.

Giles' lack of concern for anyone but Jenny is disturbing, though. He ignores Buffy, never thanks Angel, disregards Willow, Xander, and Cordelia and all the help they've given him, and instead comforts and helps out Jenny. Although, perhaps in this way he acts more like a teenager than ever before.

HIGHLIGHT: Willow yelling at Xander and Cordelia like a parent and telling them to get out of her library. Go, Willow!

NITPICKS: After seeing Philip Henry walking when he's supposed to be dead, why would Giles not tell Buffy what was really going on? Shame or no shame, he knows Buffy is strong enough to handle herself and that she and the gang will come up with a plan. Also, why didn't Giles have his tattoo removed long ago? Finally, Buffy entrusts the blood delivery to Angel, who helps her out by fighting off the vampires who were stealing it. Yet in "Angel," Darla had opened Angel's fridge to reveal those same blood packets from the hospital. So his scoffing at the vampires for stealing the blood is more than a little hypocritical.

OOPS: The Saturday computer tutorial is at 9:15 AM, but it's interrupted by Ethan and Philip. Allowing Giles time to get there, by the time Philip turns into goop and Ethan escapes, Giles and Jenny probably leave at around 10:30 AM. Why, then, is it night when they arrive at Giles' place? Also, in the computer tutorial Cordelia says the police were questioning Giles about a homicide, yet she arrived after they'd said that. How did she know what they were questioning him about?

INTERESTING FACT: This episode was rated TV 14, but it's not clear why. It contains no blood or especially gory violence.

MUSIC/BANDS: Score by Christophe Beck.

BEST POP CULTURE REFERENCE: Buffy's fantasy is having Gavin

Rossdale (from the British rock group Bush) massage her feet, while Willow dreams of John Cusack, who many consider the smart woman's sex symbol. Incidentally, Amy Yip, who is the subject of Xander's fantasy, is a Hong Kong porn actress.

2.9 What's My Line?

ORIGINAL AIR DATE: November 17, 1997
WRITTEN BY: Howard Gordon and Marti Noxon
DIRECTED BY: David Solomon

GUEST CAST: Seth Green as Oz
Bianca Lawson as Kendra
James Marsters as Spike
Juliet Landau as Drusilla
Armin Shimerman as Principal Snyder
Eric Saiek as Dalton
Kelly Connell as Norman "Worm-man" Pfister
Saviero Guerra as Willy
Michael Rothhaar as Suitman
P.B. Hutton as Mrs. Kalish

Spike orders bounty hunters to come and stop Buffy while he plans to heal Drusilla, but one of the "demons" turns out to be someone quite unexpected.

This is one of those satisfying episodes where the diehard viewer is rewarded. To understand why Kendra shows up, you had to have seen "Prophecy Girl." The book Spike is trying to decipher was acquired in "Lie to Me," when it was first stolen by another vampire. Angel asks Buffy to go skating because of the chastisement he received from Willow in "Reptile Boy," where she told him to be more direct in his relationship with Buffy.

The highlight of this episode is that spooky, ghoulish relationship between Spike and Drusilla, but it begs a very important question. If a vampire is soulless, as Angel explains, and doesn't care at all about others, why does Spike care for Dru so much? In "Surprise," the Judge will tell Spike he senses a humanity about him, so it's hard to pin him down. Dru might be mistaken for a vampire with humanity as well, but she proves that theory wrong when she starts playing with Spike's emotions later. Does Spike have a soul? Is he, perhaps, someone who was a murderer or had a sadistic personality to begin with? If so, he would be just as evil with a soul as without.

Aside from Spike and Dru, "What's My Line?" is about Buffy's future and the possibilities open to her. When everyone is taking aptitude tests to discover what career they are suited to, it hits them in a big way that slaying vampires will always be Buffy's career. How will she pay the bills? Will she be forced to get a second job? She'll be unable to have a family, Giles may die before she does, and her "slayerettes" will eventually move on to other jobs and she'll be alone. What kind of future is that? In Part Two of this episode we'll be given even harder questions to answer.

Willie the Snitch is an interesting character, but one who goes unexplained. How does he know so much about the vampire activity? Has he been Angel's source for all the information he has been passing on to Buffy? Willie's New York accent, along with the way Angel beats him up, is a humorous homage to gangster films.

This was a great lead-up to the second part of the episode, which deals with all of the issues raised in this one.

HIGHLIGHT: Willow's star treatment from the computer corporation. Canapé, anyone?

NITPICKS: If Willow suffers from "frog fear," why was she able to remove the frog's eye in "The Witch" without hesitation, and why does she carry a green stuffed frog with her ("Inca Mummy Girl")? Also, the fact that Buffy gets into situations where she must be saved by others is becoming annoying. In this episode, "School Hard," and "Angel" (to name a few), she somehow ends up on her back, her eyes grow wide as the demon hauls off to hit her, and then someone saves the day. Why does she let herself become completely helpless?

OOPS: After Kendra slams Buffy into Angel's coffee table, the remnants of the table on the floor mysteriously disappear.

MUSIC/BANDS: As Willow is wined and dined by the computer corporation, the music playing at their "booth" is the Allegro movement from "Spring," from Antonio Vivaldi's *Four Seasons*. Score by Sean Murray and Shawn Clement.

BEST POP CULTURE REFERENCE: Xander tells Cordelia, "You wanna be a member of the Scooby gang, you gotta be willing to be inconvenienced every now and then." Many people born after 1970 grew up on *Scooby-Doo*, the cartoon about a gang of crime-fighting teenagers and their dog. The leader was Freddy, the Ken-doll look-alike who drove their psychedelic van, the Mystery Machine; Daphne was the pretty one, who was fashion conscious and definitely had the hots for Freddy; Velma was the brains behind the group, the short one with glasses who usually figured out who the culprit was; and Shaggy, the hippie who took care of Scooby, was the nerdy guy who always got into trouble. In some ways there is a resemblance between our slayers and the Scooby gang, if you think about it.

2.10 What's My Line? (Part Two)

ORIGINAL AIR DATE: November 24, 1997
WRITTEN BY: Marti Noxon
DIRECTED BY: David Semel

GUEST CAST: Seth Green as Oz
Bianca Lawson as Kendra
James Marsters as Spike
Juliet Landau as Drusilla
Saviero Guerra as Willy
Kelly Connell as Norman "Worm-man" Pfister
Danny Strong as Hostage Kid

Kendra turns out to be another vampire slayer, and Giles finds out that Spike and Drusilla need Angel to help revive Drusilla.

The most baffling aspect of this episode is that Buffy doesn't jump for joy when she discovers who Kendra is. We have watched 20 episodes up to this point where Buffy has complained and pitied herself almost to the point of being tiresome, and now she's faced with an easy way out and doesn't take it. Kendra is a textbook slayer (if such a thing exists), and could probably handle the slayage on her own. Buffy has rebelled against Giles' wanting to do everything by the book, yet she is jealous when he shows genuine interest in how Kendra does all of her reading.

Willow is correct, though, when she reassures Buffy that the Sunnydale slayer will always be Giles' favorite. We soon realize that Kendra is more like a robot than a human being, and her entire life has been shaped by her calling. Kendra is like many children who show potential or an extraordinary talent, whether it be in music, sports, academics, etc. Think of any classical pianist, for example, who is world-renowned. That person has probably been playing since age two, practising three hours a day at age four, had little to no social life growing up, and is practising 12 to 15 hours a day as a professional. These people are breathtaking to watch onstage, but probably wouldn't know the difference between Marilyn Monroe and Marilyn Manson.

Similarly, Kendra has no friends, no family, no social life, and no goals other than to rid the world of vampires. She's all a slayer is supposed to be, but she sacrifices everything — including a personality — to do her duty. Her watcher won't even let her talk to guys, probably to teach her that she can't have an honest relationship, anyway. Although Kendra's slaying technique is better than Buffy's, Buffy points out that, unlike Kendra, she has emotions which help her fight harder. For proof, one need only think of "Never Kill a Boy on the First Date" and how angry Buffy became when she thought Owen had been killed. However, Buffy's emotions are a hindrance as well. Later, when Angel becomes Angelus, we'll see how Buffy's feelings for him indirectly cause a lot of grief to others.

Meanwhile, back at the bat cave, Dru tortures Angel with holy water and memories of what he'd done to her. Landau is so convincing in this scene that we realize just how insane Dru is. After she had lost her family, friends, and soul, her mind reverted back to that of a little girl. Angel becomes her new toy, and with delight she pours the holy water on him, burning his skin and causing the memories of what he did to come flooding back. The joy of torturing Angel seems to momentarily restore her strength.

The final scene is amazing. Kendra and Buffy make a great team, fighting together as an unbeatable powerhouse. They stop the ritual before it kills Angel, and Kendra surprisingly helps Buffy save Angel. So why does she return to Africa? If she has no family to return to and the hellmouth is in Sunnydale, it seems strange that she would leave. Buffy is one tough slayer, but she never would have won that fight without Kendra.

Of course, I can't close this entry without mentioning how strange and hilarious the Cordelia/Xander relationship is; this is the first episode where they start necking to the sound of violins, but they both deny there is anything between them. Thankfully, the writers develop the Oz and Willow pairing further, with Willow opening up when a guy she likes actually shows her some real attention for a change.

This episode marks a turning point in Buffy, and from now on she ceases to complain about her "job." "What's My Line? Part Two" had all the elements of a great show, and the gothic resurrection of Spike and Drusilla at the end promised us more excitement with our favorite vampires.

HIGHLIGHT: Oz talking about the stranger side of Animal Crackers.

EVERETT COLLECTION / WARNER BROS.

NITPICKS: Why do Kendra's parents know she's a slayer and Buffy's don't? More importantly, Kendra's parents gave her to her watcher when she was very young, while Buffy didn't receive her calling until she was in high school — doesn't that make Kendra the first slayer? Speaking of Kendra, that has got to be the worst accent on this show ever.

OOPS: Watch Kendra's braid in the goodbye scene with Buffy.

INTERESTING FACT: Danny Strong has become a recurring character named Jonathan, yet in the credits for this episode he's referred to as "Hostage Kid."

MUSIC/BANDS: Score by Sean Murray and Shawn Clement.

BEST POP CULTURE REFERENCE: Buffy says to Kendra, "Back off, Pink Ranger!" a reference to one of the overly hyper fighters in *The Mighty Morphin Power Rangers*. This is especially funny because Sophia Crawford, Sarah Michelle Gellar's stunt double, was also the fight double for the Pink Ranger.

2.11 Ted

ORIGINAL AIR DATE: December 8, 1997
WRITTEN BY: David Greenwalt and Joss Whedon
DIRECTED BY: Bruce Seth Green

GUEST CAST: Robia LaMorte as Jenny Calendar
John Ritter as Ted
Kristine Sutherland as Joyce Summers
Ken Thorley as Neal
James G. MacDonald as Detective Stein
Jeff Langton as Vampire

Buffy must look inside herself to try to understand why she hates her mother's new boyfriend so much.

Although "Ted" had one of the cheesiest wrap-ups of any *Buffy the Vampire Slayer* episode, the metaphor was brilliant. Ted is not only a salesman, but a guy dating Buffy's mom, and, as many children with separated parents can tell you, there is a fine line between the two. First the parent will try to sell the new person in her life to the child, telling the child how wonderful he is (Joyce skips that part because of circumstances beyond her control); then the boyfriend must sell himself, as Ted tries to do. He will ask about school, work, friends, clothes, etc., in an attempt to befriend the child, and eventually will begin sounding like a robot.

However, one of the biggest fears a child has in this situation is that the parent will take more interest in the new person than in the child. Buffy feels this angst more than many children because she has no siblings and the only people she can talk to are her friends. What makes Buffy's situation more difficult is that her friends won't listen to her, either siding with Ted or Joyce or reasoning that she's overreacting. Things get out of control when Buffy "kills" Ted and for the first time thinks she has murdered someone who wasn't a demon. Has her slaying gotten the better of her? Has she lost control of her strength to the point where she'll attack anyone who angers her? And even if she was right — she *was* defending herself against someone inflicting mental and physical abuse on her — it will be difficult for her to convince others; she's not exactly helpless. The irony of the kids all talking about this incident at school is that although they've seen her slay vampires on a nightly basis, they rationalize that and block it from their memories, yet when she kills someone in the privacy of her own home, with no witnesses but Joyce, everyone treats her like a murderer.

When Ted dies, we see the effect it has on Joyce. Children tend to rebel against their parents dating other people, yet they rarely stop to consider why their parents are dating again. Joyce has been left to raise Buffy on her own, trying to steer her in the right direction while dealing with the challenges of being a single mother. Granted, she puts up blinders when Buffy tells her Ted threatened to hit her, but Buffy is immediately rude to Joyce when she first walks in and catches them together.

One of the subtle things about this episode is the references to other episodes. "Ted" doesn't develop the characters, other than to reunite Giles and Jenny, but unlike many television series that are episodic, *Buffy the Vampire Slayer* has continuity and consistency. So Buffy, Willow, and Xander talk about how the bounty hunters were called off, Jenny says she has stayed out of mortal danger for three weeks ("The Dark Age" occurred three episodes before "Ted"), and Buffy is wrapping Angel's hand, which was stabbed in "What's My Line? Part 2."

The ending of this episode was weak. First of all, if you had killed four wives, would you be keeping them in the closet? Wouldn't the families of those women report them as missing and trace them back to Ted? Ted being a robot was strange enough; adding the serial-killer bit was just gratuitous. "Ted" had a lot of potential, and John Ritter was terrific, but the ending just fell flat.

HIGHLIGHT: The hilarious circumstance that Cordy's design sense — that the Persian rug didn't belong in Ted's room — would be the key to solving his identity.

OOPS: When the police officer asks Buffy where Ted first hit her, she points to the wrong cheek.

MUSIC/BANDS: The cheesy music playing in Ted's apartment was written especially for the scene by Los Angeles Post Music, a company that writes music for specific situations. Score by Christophe Beck.

BEST POP CULTURE REFERENCE: Xander: "Who was the real power? The Captain or Tennille?" The Captain and Tennille — Daryl Dragon and Toni Tennille — were a husband-and-wife duo who had several hits in the late 1970s, including "Do That To Me One More Time" and "The Way I Want To Touch You." Tennille made several solo albums in the 1980s, and has appeared on Broadway.

2.12 Bad Eggs

ORIGINAL AIR DATE: January 12, 1998
WRITTEN BY: Marti Noxon
DIRECTED BY: David Greenwalt

GUEST CAST: Kristine Sutherland as Joyce Summers
Jeremy Ratchford as Lyle Gorch
James Parks as Tector Gorch
Rick Zieff as Mr. Whitmore
Danny Strong as Jonathan
Brie McCaddin as Cute Girl
Eric Whitmore as Night Watchman

When Buffy and the gang are given eggs as part of a typical high school parenting project, their eggs become more of a burden than they could have imagined.

Even a fantastic show like *Buffy the Vampire Slayer* is going to have a bad episode once in a while. "Bad Eggs" is not one of my favorites, to say the least: it is a meandering and confused episode that attempts to offer up a metaphor for teen pregnancy. The metaphor is unclear, though, and begs a lot of questions, such as, What exactly

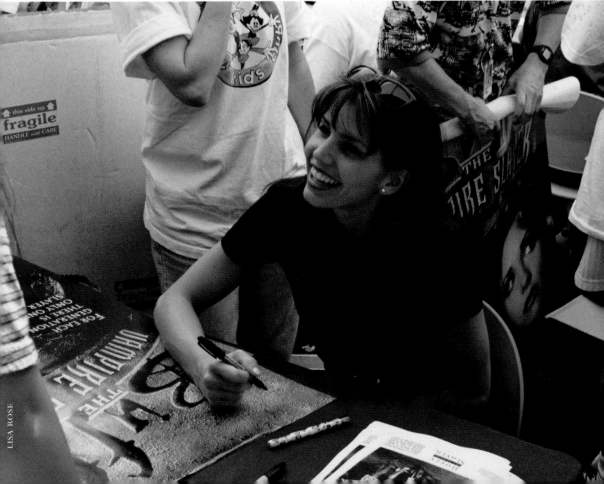

is that octopus creature supposed to represent? Why is it under the school? How did the health teacher get caught in its spell?

If you really stretch, you can work out some idea of what the show is trying to convey. The sex ed teacher gives the students an egg to carry around, and the students must follow a checklist — feed it, burp it, and diaper it. Considering you can't literally do any of those things with an egg, most students do what Buffy does — check off each of the points before going to bed. This exercise in futility is precisely what makes it meaningless: it has no bearing on the reality of having children. Only when Willow and Buffy are under the spell of the egg do the burdens of teen pregnancy kick in. They become slaves to it, are tired and sluggish during the day, infect those around them (imagine how many teenagers ask their parents to baby sit their child), and turn into zombies. To top it off, in many cases the male takes no responsibility (hence Xander boiling his "child").

If that explanation is indeed what the writers were trying to convey, then it was an intelligent comparison, but the main plot fell flat. The little creatures in the eggs were ridiculous, and the subplot of the Texan vampires seemed tacked on so we wouldn't forget Buffy is actually a *vampire* slayer. However, the Texan vampires were far more interesting than the eggs, and this is the only time we've seen vampire siblings on the show.

The relationship between Buffy and her mother is used as a weak parallel for Buffy and her egg, but when Joyce hears Buffy on the phone she goes completely ballistic for no apparent reason. She's caught Buffy doing far more suspicious things, so her anger makes no sense, other than as a contrived way to show how tough parenting can be when you're dealing with an unruly teenager.

One of the few reasons to watch this episode at all is for the great make-out sessions between Buffy and Angel. Their relationship is getting hotter, which offers the perfect lead-in to "Surprise" and "Innocence."

HIGHLIGHT: Cordelia's rant about her bear knapsack.

NITPICKS: After Buffy kills the mother creature, the squiggly creature detaches itself from Willow's back. Why don't we see the creatures falling from everyone else's back? Shouldn't they be all over the floor?

OOPS: As Buffy fights with Lyle in the arcade, they collide with the pinball machine that a girl was playing moments before, yet the machine doesn't appear to be turned on.

MUSIC/BANDS: As Buffy and Joyce are shopping at the mall, you can hear selections from Mozart's *Eine Kleine Nachtmusik* and *Die Zauberflote*. Score by Clement and Murray.

BEST POP CULTURE REFERENCE: Lyle and Tector Gorch are the names of two of the meanest members of the marauding gang in Sam Peckinpah's 1969 film *The Wild Bunch*, although Lyle was the smaller of the two. (See "The Harvest" for more explanation.)

2.13 Surprise (Part One)

ORIGINAL AIR DATE: January 19, 1998
WRITTEN BY: Marti Noxon
DIRECTED BY: Michael Lange

GUEST CAST: Seth Green as Oz
Kristine Sutherland as Joyce Summers
Robia LaMorte as Jenny Calendar
Brian Thompson as The Judge
Eric Saiet as Dalton
Mercedes MacNab as Harmony
Vincent Schiavelli as Enyos (Jenny's Uncle)
James Marsters as Spike
Juliet Landau as Drusilla

Drusilla and Spike reassemble the Judge, which will bring about Armageddon, and Angel and Buffy try to stop them. Meanwhile, we discover that Jenny has been harboring a dark secret.

"Surprise" was mind-blowing, it was so good. The WB was kind enough to air "Surprise" and "Innocence" on consecutive nights when it first aired, so audiences weren't forced to wait a week to discover exactly what happened to everyone. The episode opens with Buffy's dream, which has got to be one of the most realistic dream sequences ever filmed. Nothing makes sense, everything is disconnected, some elements are events that have actually happened to Buffy and others are prophetic, showing what will happen. The scene was absolutely brilliant.

It is interesting that the writers have set up a parallel between Drusilla and Buffy. In her dream, Buffy sees Dru killing Angel.

However, it will be Buffy who inadvertently "kills" Angel and resurrects Angelus. Both Buffy and Dru have parties — Buffy's birthday falls at the same time as Dru's coming-out party — and both of them are the leaders of their separate gangs. Spike is trapped in a wheelchair and is clearly furious with his lack of abilities, just as Xander has always resented that he must step aside while Buffy does all the fighting. Eventually Angelus will make Spike as jealous as he'd once made Xander.

We discover the gang has a traitor in their midst in the unlikely person of Jenny. She is actually Janna of the Kalderash gypsy clan, which adds a fascinating twist to the story line. Gypsies originated in northern India, but through centuries of massacre and persecution they have scattered all over the world. The Kalderash gypsies, who are from the Balkans and are found mostly in central Europe, are the most numerous. Because gypsies were a migratory people, they were renowned for bringing new inventions, ideas, and their own folklore to other people. What makes a gypsy element in *Buffy the Vampire Slayer* so interesting is that much of the vampire and werewolf folklore originated with the gypsies. They have a rich oral tradition, and their language is Romani, a highly inflected tongue that likely descended from Sanskrit.

Many of the gypsies' oral stories reflect their anger after years of persecution and misunderstanding. Throughout history, gypsies have been blamed for strange occurrences and subsequently banished from the areas in which they stopped and set up camp.

Within the tribal groups, nothing is more revered than loyalty and cohesiveness, which explains Enyos' anger when he accuses Jenny of forgetting her people. Technological advances and urban culture are the biggest concerns to gypsies, who feel that these outside forces may threaten their lifestyle, and Jenny is a computer-science teacher who seems to have embraced urban culture. The other threat to the gypsy culture is intermarriage with non-gypsies. Thus, Jenny is torn between her loyalty to and love for a people that have raised her and provided her with a belief system, and the duty she feels toward her friends and the man she loves. Faced with probable banishment, she must act and keep Buffy away from Angel — but it's too late. We sympathize with Jenny, but at the same time she is responsible for not having told Buffy about the "one moment of true happiness" bit.

The scene with Buffy and Angel at the docks is beautifully executed by both actors, and even viewers who are no longer teenagers will recognize how difficult it is for these lovers to be separated for any amount of time, much less three months. The acting by Sarah and David in this scene will be surpassed only in the season finale. This was a wonderful, heartbreaking episode that must have had every Buffy fan on the edge of their seats waiting for its conclusion the following night.

HIGHLIGHT: Oz's reaction to seeing the vampire get staked.

NITPICKS: Why does the bookworm vampire wear glasses? Aren't a vampire's senses supposed to be heightened?

INTERESTING FACT: The Judge is played by the same actor who was Luke in "The Harvest." Also, in Buffy's first dream, Willow says to the monkey in French, "L'hippo a piqué tes pantalons," which is a very slang way of saying, "The hippo has stolen your pants." This is probably a reference to the Animal Cracker discussion she and Oz had in "What's My Line? Part Two." (Oz had said the hippo was jealous of the monkey's pants and that all monkeys were French.) Obviously Willow has told Buffy about the conversation for it to have made its way into Buffy's subconscious. Also, on August 30, 1998, *Buffy the Vampire Slayer* won the Technical Emmy for Best Makeup for a Series for the work done in "Surprise/Innocence."

MUSIC/BANDS: This episode was scored by Christophe Beck. The song in the dream sequence is called "Anything," written by Sean Murray and Shawn Clement. When Angel tells Buffy he loves her, "Angel/Buffy Theme" is playing. During Drusilla's party the song she cues is "Transylvanian Concubine" by the wonderfully ghoulish group Rasputina, from their *Thanks for the Ether* album.

2.14 Innocence (Part Two)

ORIGINAL AIR DATE: January 20, 1998
WRITTEN BY: Joss Whedon
DIRECTED BY: Joss Whedon

GUEST CAST: Seth Green as Oz
Robia LaMorte as Jenny Calendar
Kristine Sutherland as Joyce Summers
Brian Thompson as The Judge
Ryan Francis as Soldier
Vincent Schiavelli as Enyos
James Marsters as Spike
Juliet Landau as Drusilla
James Lurie as Teacher

Buffy must deal with the fact that Angel has become the evil Angelus, and she must stop the Judge.

If "Surprise" brought a lump to your throat, then "Innocence" probably induced a wave of tears. This episode was an extraordinary blending of main plot and metaphor, showing one of the possible aftermaths of teen sex. Buffy is devastated when Angel acts indifferent and crass after they had made love the night before, and as her face mirrors the emotions coursing through her, we watch her heart break before us. After 25 episodes of Angel being the good guy, the writers immediately challenge our sensibilities, turning us against him in an instant (I mean, the guy won't even *call* her!). Boreanaz is brilliant as the evil Angelus, exceeding the work he'd done before as the good guy.

"Innocence" was a powerful episode about the complexity of relationships. In early scenes you can tell Cordelia is hurt that Xander still insults her in front of the gang. When Xander apologizes, it's the first time he and Cordy have come to an understanding about something, and their relationship takes a tiny step beyond simply being a gropefest. Willow catches them kissing for the first time and is devastated, yet she has just begun dating Oz! Meanwhile, imagine how Cordelia must feel as Xander chases after Willow, insisting that Cordelia means nothing to him. Buffy is trapped in a post-coital bewilderment, Giles finds out the truth about Jenny and the discovery causes a rift between them, and Oz senses that Willow cares for Xander and refuses to move the relationship forward until he's certain that she cares for him more. Whew! Who ever said love was easy?

One of the great aspects of this episode was how Buffy acts the day after she loses her virginity. Joyce recognizes a strange look on Buffy's face, and Buffy seems to be covering something up. Like many girls, Buffy feels as though the loss of her virginity is stamped on her forehead and everyone will know. Only Willow senses what has happened, and she is sympathetic. Giles, too, will discover the secret, and will look appropriately flustered. Meanwhile, in other relationships, when Angelus enters the demonic fold of Drusilla and Spike they are both happy to see him, but Spike has no idea what he's in for. Angel will be far more problematic to Spike without a soul than he ever was before.

We instantly recognize what Angel is capable of doing. Where other vampires hunt because of their desire for blood, Angelus plays with the minds of his victims, torturing them for long periods of time. In other words, his return isn't an immediate threat to Buffy, but to all of her closest friends. As he puts it, he will kill her from the inside, rather than taking the pain away by killing her quickly. Buffy, on the other hand, is left with a material reminder of him — the Claddagh ring.

The creator of the Claddagh ring was Richard Joyce of Galway, who was on his way to a life of slavery on a West Indies plantation when he was captured by pirates and sold to a goldsmith. There Joyce learned the craft, and when he returned to Galway in 1689 he designed the Claddagh ring. If the wearer of the ring wears it on the right hand with the heart facing out, then he or she is free; worn with the crown out means that person is spoken for; and worn on the left hand with the crown out means the wearer is destined to be with his or her love forever. For that reason, Claddagh rings are often used as wedding bands. The heart symbolizes love, the crown loyalty, and the hands friendship. The right hand that holds the heart is supposed to belong to Dagda, the father of the gods of the Tuatha dé Danaan, a group of deities in Irish myth who were eventually conquered and became fairies. The left hand belongs to Anu, the mother of the Celts in ancient Celtic lore. The Claddagh ring has become popular worldwide, although it is fitting that we later discover Angel, too, is from Galway.

Although Buffy's failure to kill Angelus at the end of "Innocence" will lead to immense guilt over the repercussions, we can't blame her. She let herself fall in love with a vampire, true, but many teenage girls fall for people they shouldn't, and no matter how badly she's treated, it's difficult for the girl to let him go.

The best part of this episode is the talk Buffy and Giles have in his car at the end. Giles tells her all the things teenagers long to hear from their parents but rarely do. He tells her he respects her and doesn't blame her for failing to kill Angel. However, his talk sounds a little *too* passionate — he agrees Buffy fell in with the wrong person, that Angel turned out not to be who everyone thought he was, but that she's not to blame for falling in love with him. Clearly, Giles also has Jenny in mind. Regardless, this was a wonderful scene, and I was disappointed only that it didn't end with a hug (although that would have been very un-Giles-like). "Innocence" was an amazing experience and definitely in the top five episodes of the season.

HIGHLIGHT: Willow's explanation to Oz of why they're stealing a rocket launcher: "Well, we don't have cable, so we have to make our own fun."

NITPICKS: Drusilla tortures Angel in "What's My Line? Part Two" for what he did to her family, yet now that the demon itself is standing before her, she couldn't be happier. Is this a character inconsistency, or a further indication that Dru has completely lost her mind? Also, if a 5'3" girl stood on a jewelry counter in a crowded mall and shot off a rocket launcher, causing this huge blue creature to explode into tiny pieces, don't you think that would be a *little* difficult to cover up?

OOPS: Big continuity error. When Buffy goes home and cries herself to sleep, Willow, Xander, Oz, and Cordelia are getting together to break into the army barracks. Buffy wakes up, realizes Jenny knows the truth, and goes to school to force the truth out of her. *Then* we get the scene where the gang breaks into the army barracks *the night before*. Major oops.

INTERESTING FACT: The first time this episode aired, it garnered 5.2, the highest Nielsen rating ever on *Buffy the Vampire Slayer*. In other words, over five million households were tuned in to the show.

MUSIC/BANDS: Score by Christophe Beck.

BEST POP CULTURE REFERENCE: Buffy tells the others to watch the exits and leave the Judge to her: "I'll handle the Smurf." This is a reference to *The Smurfs* (1981–1989), a children's cartoon that featured a colony of tiny blue creatures who lived in a mushroom village, avoiding the evil wizard Gargamel.

2.15 Phases

ORIGINAL AIR DATE: January 27, 1998
WRITTEN BY: Rob Des Hotel and Dean Batali
DIRECTED BY: Bruce Seth Green

GUEST CAST: Seth Green as Oz
Camila Griggs as the Gym Teacher
Jack Conley as Cain
Larry Bagby III as Larry
Megahn Perry as Theresa Klusmeyer
Keith Campbell as Werewolf

When a werewolf begins attacking people making out in Lover's Lane, Oz thinks he might be the creature.

So far we've had vampires, mummies, demonic possession, witches, monsters, even squiggly things popping out of eggs, so werewolves were inevitable. "Phases" takes on the werewolf legend with conventions from different werewolf movies.

The werewolf legend first became popular in Europe, and between 1520 and 1630 it developed into mass hysteria. In France alone there were over 30,000 wolf trials, and as was the case with the witch trials, many of the accused were poor peasants. When people began dying or crops failed, it was blamed on werewolves who were believed to be wandering at night, just as vampires have been blamed. By some reports, the werewolf could shape change at will, but by others it was beyond the person's control.

The fact that Oz can't remember anything about the werewolf is a strange twist to the mythology. According to legend, even if the person doesn't realize he is a werewolf while he is transformed, usually something will happen during the day that triggers his memory, and the events come flooding back. In fact, it is those very memories that make the existence of a werewolf so horrible — the person must live with graphic knowledge of his crimes, unable to stop them. No chains or prison can hold a werewolf, either, because he possesses superhuman strength. In other words, the gang's acceptance of Oz's condition ignores some very important elements of the lore, like how once a month Willow's life will be in real danger.

As with vampirism, throughout history there have been psychiatric reports of people believing they are werewolves. This phenomenon is called lycanthropy, after the king Lycaon, who was turned into a wolf by Zeus. In most cases where the patient shows lycanthropic tendencies or beliefs, they are diagnosed with paranoid schizophrenia. Sometimes drug use is involved and the patients hallucinate, or there is an extreme mental disorder.

According to folklore, there are various signs that suggest a person might be a werewolf (you can use the following list to check out your friends): having hairy palms or an extremely long index or middle finger; sleeping often because of the exhaustion brought on by his transformation; sleeping with his mouth open because he can't unclench his jaws once closed; often having a pentagram somewhere on his body that mysteriously appears after the first kill. There are also several ways to become a werewolf: eating wolf or human flesh; eating the brain of a wolf; being bitten by a wolf or werewolf; being born on Christmas; and on and on. The only way to kill a werewolf is by using a silver bullet (and this method seems to be consistent in both fiction and folklore). In the folklore it is believed a werewolf becomes a vampire when it dies.

In werewolf films, many folklore beliefs have been altered. Oz's condition has more in common with Michael Landon's in *I Was a Teenage Werewolf* (1957) and Michael J. Fox's in *Teen Wolf* (1985), where becoming a werewolf is a metaphor for the changes a male body goes through during puberty. Even Willow spots this parallel when she compares Oz's condition to female menstruation (making every male viewer squirm). Unlike the creatures in movies, though, Oz resembles an actual wolf — which is consistent with the folklore — rather than a wolfman, the more common approach. (*An American Werewolf in London* [1981] is one of the few films that portrays werewolves as wolves.) Also, where in the folklore a person becomes a werewolf through outside circumstances, in *Teen Wolf* Fox's character inherits the tendency from his father. Similarly, Oz's suspicions about the source of his own affliction are confirmed when he discovers his cousin is a werewolf. But he didn't inherit the condition; his cousin had bitten him.

It's interesting that the writers chose to do an episode that focused on Oz right after airing "Surprise," which was the pivotal episode of the second season. It was a daring move, but a clever one. The last four episodes have either focused on the relationship between Angel and Buffy or at least used it as a major subplot, and there are fans who don't actually care about them as much as they care about other characters. So it was the perfect time to switch gears and focus on another couple for a change.

Not only does the relationship between Oz and Willow develop, but after referring to Cordelia as a "skanky ho," Willow actually connects with her for the first time, as they sit and complain about their boyfriends to one another. The very fact that Cordelia is complaining about Xander proves she no longer sees him as just a kissing toy — she's thinking of him more as a boyfriend.

There were some great references to the first season in this episode, which fans who didn't see the first season might have missed. For example, Oz watches the cheerleading trophy and comments how the eyes seem to watch him back. You would have to have seen "The Witch" to understand the joke there (Amy's mom is actually trapped inside the trophy). His comment also foreshadows the next episode, though, where Amy returns as an integral character. More importantly, there is a reference to "The Pack," where Xander slips and Buffy realizes he remembers everything he did while possessed by a hyena. Unlike the bewilderment he expressed at the end of "The Pack," here he sees the possession as something that gave him power.

"Phases" was a strong episode that not only gave us a better look at Oz, but also explored the various relationships on the show and marked the beginning of Angelus's torture of Buffy.

HIGHLIGHT: Buffy attempting to play the weak girl in self-defense class.

NITPICKS: Buffy had just signed the funeral guest book when Theresa turns into a vampire and she must stake her. Considering there is no longer a body in the casket, wouldn't Theresa's family question Buffy if she was clearly the last person to see her?

OOPS: When Xander and Cordy are in the car arguing at the beginning, watch the left side of her bangs — they keep going up and down. However, the biggest continuity error of the show happens in the library right after Giles has loaded the tranquilizer gun. As the camera changes angles, watch how the glasses keep appearing and disappearing on his face. Major oops.

MUSIC/BANDS: As Cordelia and Willow complain about their respective boyfriends at The Bronze, Lotion is performing "Blind for Now" onstage. The song is from their CD *Nobody's Cool*. Score by Shawn Clement and Sean Murray.

BEST POP CULTURE REFERENCE: Cordy says to Xander, "I think you splashed on just a little too much Obsession for Dorks," a reference to Calvin Klein's cologne Obsession for Men.

2.16 Bewitched, Bothered and Bewildered

ORIGINAL AIR DATE: February 10, 1998
WRITTEN BY: Marti Noxon
DIRECTED BY: James A. Contner

GUEST CAST: Seth Green as Oz
Kristine Sutherland as Joyce Summers
Robia LaMorte as Jenny Calendar
Elizabeth Anne Allen as Amy
Mercedes McNab as Harmony
Lorna Scott as Miss Beakman
James Marsters as Spike
Juliet Landau as Drusilla
Jason Hall as Devon
Jennie Chester as Kate

A love spell that Xander intends for Cordelia backfires, with disastrous results.

"Bewitched, Bothered and Bewildered" (the title comes from a song in the 1940 musical *Pal Joey*) was a lot of fun, and it was exciting to see a first-season guest star return. The only disappointment is that after seeing what black magic did to her mother, why would Amy cast immoral spells? (See "The Witch.") You would think Amy would be suffering from some sort of trauma after losing her mother in such a violent fashion, but instead she seems to be following in Mommy Dearest's footsteps. Love spells are actually the most frequently requested form of magic, but as mentioned in the episode-guide entry for "The Witch," if the spell is impure, its implications can backfire on the witch threefold. Hence Amy's initial hesitation to carry out Xander's request.

Even when an episode of *Buffy the Vampire Slayer* features a self-contained story, rather than one that depends on an ongoing story line (like "Innocence"), the writers still insert details to keep the action continuous with previous and future episodes. In this case, we discover Angel is especially vicious on Valentine's Day. Unfortunately, he seems to anticipate that Giles and Buffy will discover that fact and he waits until "Passion" to wreak havoc on the lives of everyone around Buffy.

Why doesn't Amy's love spell work? Perhaps she hasn't matured enough as a witch. Giles believes it's because she used Cordelia's necklace and it somehow protected her. However, it could also have had something to do with the goddess to whom Amy chants — Diana, whom she says is the goddess of love and the hunt. However, it is Venus who is the goddess of love. In addition to being the patron of wild beasts, Diana is also the goddess of childbirth. She had several temples which were presided over by priests, and what makes her temples stand out from those of other goddesses is the rite of succession from one priest to another. To become a priest of Diana's temples, one had to kill one's predecessor in hand-to-hand combat. Human sacrifices were also accepted on her altar. But there was no Roman goddess of love and compassion until Venus came along. So when Amy prays to Diana, she is praying to the goddess of the hunt, which would explain why Xander becomes hunted, not loved.

For the vengeance spells, Amy calls on the goddess Hecate, who was originally a kind goddess who promoted goodwill. However, gradually Hecate became associated with magic and sorcery, and would appear to magicians with a torch in her hand. She is credited with inventing sorcery, and statues of her were erected at cross-roads, where offerings were left for her. Amy got it right, then, when she invoked Hecate.

One of the highlights of this episode is the huge step that Cordelia takes by telling off her friends so she can be with Xander. Suddenly we realize that she sees him as more than just a toy, that she cares about his feelings. Although she and Xander will still argue as usual, this is a big step for her to take, putting them on a new course toward having an actual relationship. "Bewildered, Bothered and Bewitched" was a lot of fun, and perhaps the funniest episode of Season Two.

HIGHLIGHT: The Buffy rat.

NITPICKS: When Xander has that strut down the school hallway, even the guys are giving him looks. If that spell has affected *everybody*, including the males, why isn't Oz, Giles, or Angel affected? Speaking of Giles, it's a given that Xander has done a stupid thing, but why is Giles so angry with him? It's not like Giles never conjured up a demon like, oh, I don't know . . . Eyghon?!

OOPS: Xander and Cordelia run away from the school in the morning, yet when they arrive at Buffy's house it's evening and Joyce is at home. Exactly how far do these people live from the school?

MUSIC/BANDS: As Xander waits for Cordelia to arrive at The Bronze, the music playing is Four Star Mary's "Pain," from their self-titled CD (again, they are the band to which Dingoes Ate My Baby are lip-synching). Cordy breaks up with Xander to "Drift Away," by Naked, from their self-titled album. As Xander does his strut down the halls of Sunnydale, the hilariously appropriate "Got the Love" is playing, from the Average White Band's self-titled album. Score by Christophe Beck.

BEST POP CULTURE REFERENCE: When Xander walks down the hall to that loud music, the camera begins with his feet and moves up his body. This is a cinematic reference to the opening shot of *Saturday Night Fever* (1977), where the camera follows Travolta's feet as he walks down the street to the sounds of the Bee Gees' "Stayin' Alive" and slowly moves up his body.

ORIGINAL AIR DATE: February 24, 1998
WRITTEN BY: Ty King
DIRECTED BY: Michael E. Gershman

GUEST CAST: Kristine Sutherland as Joyce Summers
Robia LaMorte as Jenny Calendar
Richard Assad as Shop Owner
James Marsters as Spike
Juliet Landau as Drusilla
Danny Strong as Student
Richard Hoyt Miller as Policeman

Jenny tries to decipher the restoration spell to bring back Angel's soul, but Angel gets to her before she can induce it.

"Passion" is one of those gems of an episode that makes watching television worthwhile. With its subtleties in acting, music, and direction, "Passion" definitely ranks highly on any fan's list of favorites. Usually the voice-over narration in movies is a distraction, jolting the viewer out of the story and reminding her that she's watching something that isn't real. Think, for instance, of the annoying narrator in the commercially released version of *Blade Runner*, who basically tells you what is going on, as opposed to the superior director's cut of *Blade Runner*, which, without the voice-over, is a far more powerful movie.

However, Angel's voice-over in "Passion" is perfect, representing the random thoughts brought on by events as they happen (this device will be used with the same effect in the "Becoming" episodes). Everything the characters do on the series is driven by passion — Giles' love of books, Xander and Cordy in the utility closet, Willow trying to make Xander jealous, Oz's love of music, Buffy's inability to kill Angel. As the narrator says, passion is what drives us and makes us who we are. At the beginning of the episode, Giles tells Buffy she doesn't have the luxury of letting her passion rule her, yet that's like telling her she doesn't have the luxury of breathing. Buffy's only human, and she doesn't *let* her passion rule her; it just does. Even Angel is ruled by passion — his passion for torturing Buffy. Passion can be good or bad, leading us to both follow our goals and do things we regret.

Although previous episodes have merely hinted at the evil acts Angel has committed in the past, now he begins Buffy's real torture, sneaking into the rooms of people she loves and watching them while they sleep. For the first time Buffy wants to tell Joyce she's a slayer so her mother will be aware of the imminent danger lurking about. By using Giles' spell, she doesn't have to, but Joyce does find out that Buffy lost her virginity to Angel, which, for a teenage girl, is a far worse revelation. She is reminded that she created Angelus out of her own passion (a concept resolved in "I Only Have Eyes For You"), and poor Joyce must give Buffy The Talk, not realizing Buffy is mature far beyond her years. Like most mothers, Joyce fails to grasp that no matter how close a mother and daughter are, there are some things a daughter must keep to herself.

Unbeknownst to the gang, Jenny has quietly been suffering the guilt of lying to them, and decides to use her gypsy knowledge against her own people's wishes. The scene where she squares off against Angel is full of suspense, yet shocking when he actually does kill her. How many other television shows kill off a main character?

Boreanaz is absolutely frightening, acting in a whimsical fashion right before every kill. Even more amazing is Anthony Stewart Head's performance in the scene where he finds Jenny in his apartment. The only reason Giles will survive the physical torture he endures in "Becoming" is because nothing could be worse than what happens here. As he walks up the stairs, his face moves from surprise to anticipation to shock at what he finds. The music playing on the phonograph adds the final touch to a perfect scene.

In the end, Buffy is overwhelmed with guilt, but Giles won't blame her because he succumbed to his own passion by hunting down Angel. However, this episode immediately recalls Buffy's failure in "Innocence," and for the first time Xander goes beyond his jealousy of Angel and insists that he be killed. For its moral dilemmas alone, this episode stands above the rest. In my opinion, "Passion" ranks with the "Becoming" episodes as the best of the season.

HIGHLIGHT: Cordy's obsession that she let Angel in her car.

NITPICKS: Why does Jenny's tombstone read Jennifer Calendar? They all know that's not her real name. Just before Willow finds the fishkabob Angel left for her, she puts fish food in her aquarium. Wouldn't she have noticed it was empty? And how did Angel get into Giles' house if he's never been invited in? Are we to assume that he's been in Giles' apartment off-screen? Finally, another nitpick about time. Giles and Jenny make plans to meet at his house, and he leaves her in the computer science room, dropping by Buffy's house momentarily before heading home. Meanwhile, Angel talks to Jenny, chases her through the school, kills her, takes her body to

Giles's house, chills some champagne, arranges flowers, puts on the music, lights numerous candles, *and* draws a picture of Jenny's corpse before Giles gets home. Did Giles's car break down somewhere?

OOPS: Jenny asks Angel how he got into the school, yet she'd stopped him in the hallway in "Innocence," has seen him in the school numerous times, and knows that vampires can enter public places. Finally, when the gang meets in the library first thing in the morning, the clock over Giles' shoulder reads 12 o'clock.

MUSIC/BANDS: As the gang dances at The Bronze while we hear the Angel voice-over at the beginning, the song is "Never An Easy Way," performed by Morcheeba, from their album *Who Can You Trust?* When Giles enters his apartment and expects to find Jenny upstairs, that soaring music is "O soave fanciulla!" from Puccini's *La Bohème*. Christophe Beck wrote the wonderful score to this episode, and at the end, when Giles lays the flowers on Jenny's grave, you can hear Anthony Stewart Head singing.

BEST POP CULTURE REFERENCE: Xander says to Buffy, "If Giles wants to go after the fiend that killed his girlfriend, then I say, faster pussycat, kill, kill." Xander's reference is a little skewed, for Giles isn't exactly reminiscent of anyone in the film *Faster Pussycat, Kill! Kill!*, a 1965 Russ Meyer flick that garnered a cult following with its 1995 re-release. The movie is about three large-breasted, leather-clad, vicious women (the typical characters in any Russ Meyer film) who go on a murderous rampage in the desert. John Waters (*Hairspray, Pink Flamingos*) called it the best movie of all time.

2.18 Killed By Death

ORIGINAL AIR DATE: March 3, 1998
WRITTEN BY: Rob Des Hotel and Dean Batali
DIRECTED BY: Deran Serafian

GUEST CAST: Kristine Sutherland as Joyce Summers
Richard Herd as Dr. Backer
Willie Garson as Security Guard
Andrew Ducote as Ryan
Juanita Jennings as Dr. Wilkinson
Robert Munic as Intern
Mimi Paley as Young Buffy

Denise Johnson as Celia
James Jude Courtney as Kindestod

Buffy discovers at the hospital that Death is materializing into a monster and killing the children.

It would have been tough to top "Passion," and unfortunately "Killed By Death" doesn't even come close. The only interesting aspects were the subplots — the main story line was too episodic and looked more like filler than anything else.

Given that, it was a great episode for fans of the Xander/Cordy relationship. Cordelia finally tells Xander straight out that she's sick and tired of him paying more attention to Buffy than he does to her. Cordelia's character has weathered a lot of changes this season, although the essential Cordy self-centeredness is still there. She has gone from being a vicious, snobby, selfish cheerleader to someone who cares more about her friends than about her own popularity. In this episode, there is a subtle moment that speaks volumes where she brings Xander a bag of doughnuts. She knows he's guarding Buffy's door, but she cares about him enough to get him something to eat.

This episode also featured the only face-off between Angelus and Xander, and Xander discovers that Buffy and Angel slept together. Angel rubs it in his face, making Xander feel like the lesser man. Nonetheless, Xander holds his ground and forces Angel to leave, reminding him that he'll never be mortal. Xander will do and say some pretty questionable things in upcoming episodes, but we have to keep in mind that he probably has Buffy's well-being first and foremost in his mind.

Buffy's flashbacks to her cousin's death were illuminating, and the fact that when Buffy was a child she played the superhero is very funny. Kindestod itself is a cross between Freddie Krueger and the Penguin, but if there was a metaphor here, it was buried pretty deep in the story line. It's obvious the writers are offering a possible explanation of mysterious child deaths, but what does that have to do with the gang?

"Killed By Death" was uneventful overall, and the biggest shame is that when it originally aired, a seven-week hiatus of repeats followed it. The writers weren't exactly tiding us over with this one.

HIGHLIGHT: Willow using her frog fear to distract the security guards.

NITPICKS: At the beginning, the gang throws a jacket over Angel's head to stop his attack on Buffy. Why didn't somebody stake him?

Also, if Buffy is tougher than most people on account of being the slayer, how can the flu cause her to pass out?

OOPS: Kindestod disappears through a door marked Basement Access, but that sign wasn't there in previous scenes. Also, the doughnuts Cordelia buys for Xander are from Krispy Kreme, but there are no Krispy Kreme outlets in California.

MUSIC/BANDS: Score by Christophe Beck.

BEST POP CULTURE REFERENCE: After Buffy says she's going to fight Death, Xander tells her, "If he asks you to play chess, don't even do it; he's a whiz." Xander is alluding to the 1957 Ingmar Bergman film *The Seventh Seal*, where a knight challenges Death to a game of chess in order to get his life back. That scenario has been parodied in numerous films and television shows since, including *The Dove* (1968), where Death is challenged to a game of one-point badminton, *Bill and Ted's Bogus Journey* (1991), where the boys try to beat Death in Clue, Woody Allen's *Love and Death* (1975), and even *The Animaniacs*, where Yakko, Wakko, and Dot beat Death at a game of checkers.

2.19 I Only Have Eyes For You

ORIGINAL AIR DATE: April 28, 1998
WRITTEN BY: Marti Noxon
DIRECTED BY: James Whitmore, Jr.

GUEST STARS: James Marsters as Spike
Juliet Landau as Drusilla
Armin Shimerman as Principal Snyder
Meredith Salenger as Grace Newman
Christopher Gorham as James Stanley
John Hawkes as George
Miriam Flynn as Ms. Frank
Brian Reddy as Police Chief Bob
Brian Poth as Fighting Boy
Sarah Bibb as Fighting Girl
James Lurie as Mr. Miller
Ryan Taszreak as Ben

A poltergeist is haunting Sunnydale High, forcing people to repeatedly re-enact a murder that happened over 40 years ago.

After seven weeks of going into Buffy Withdrawal Syndrome, "I Only Have Eyes For You" was a brilliant way to return to the show. We discover that Buffy feels guilty not because she couldn't kill Angel at the mall, but because she was the catalyst that took away his soul. When the gang discovers that the poltergeist haunting the school killed his teacher out of love, Buffy becomes furious and immediately turns on him. The fact that he will eventually use her to get out of his purgatory should come as no shock.

The way the death scene is played out over and over never gets tiring — as we watch four couples do it (including the original one, in a flashback), it's interesting to see how each adapts to the scenario; only Buffy and Angel switch gender roles. The other exciting aspect of this episode is that the guest stars are recognizable faces. Meredith Salenger starred in numerous 1980s teen films opposite such names as River Phoenix (*A Night in the Life of Jimmy Reardon*), Corey Haim, and Corey Feldman (*Dream a Little Dream*). Miriam Flynn has appeared frequently in television and movie roles, and is best known as cousin Catherine in the *National Lampoon's Vacation* movies. "Go Fish" will feature Conchata Ferrell, who has been in dozens of television and movie roles, including that of the wisecracking entertainment lawyer, Susan Bloom, in *LA Law* for a season. *Buffy*'s popularity has obviously made it the show people want to be on.

Giles's reaction to the poltergeist is sad — he so wants Jenny to return that he believes she is trying to contact him through paranormal activity. His inability to accept any other explanation forces the gang to find out for themselves what is really going on, and even as they are carrying out their plan, Willow can't bring herself to tell Giles his assumptions are misdirected. Only when the activity escalates to the point of putting their lives in danger does he admit to himself that he must be wrong.

"I Only Have Eyes For You" has some essential developments. First of all, Spike clearly preferred Angel when he had a soul, although Spike didn't realize it at the time. Angel tortures Spike with as much glee as when he's torturing Buffy, and in this episode he and Drusilla flirt in front of Spike, who is still in his wheelchair. Angel's handicap jokes escalate, and Drusilla doesn't seem to care about Spike's feelings at all, although we can't forget that she has no soul and *couldn't* care about him. Spike's jealousy and anger, though, once again reinforce the notion he's different from most vampires, who don't seem to show emotion.

Also, we discover that Snyder knows about the hellmouth, although he seems to be in the dark about Buffy being the slayer. The mention of city council bringing him in as principal would explain his hatred for the students — he's probably not a principal at all.

The love scene between Buffy and Angel is beautifully acted, especially by Boreanaz, who is playing a woman. He displays feminine gestures without ever playing it over the top. For a brief moment, it appears as though we have the old Angel back. In acting out the scene, Buffy is able to put her conscience at ease, for just as Grace was able to forgive James, Angel tells Buffy, "I loved you with my last breath," and we know that he means it.

This one was a tearjerker, and a great setup for the season finale.

HIGHLIGHT: Spike getting out of his wheelchair. Woo-hoo!

NITPICKS: Why have we never heard that bell tower before? Also, there's no way the students are blind enough to believe Snyder's "backed-up sewer" explanation for the sudden appearance of snakes on their trays.

OOPS: Willow mentions Jenny's lesson plans and bookmarks on her computer. Did the writers somehow forget the bonfire Angel made with Jenny's hard drive? Also, "I Only Have Eyes For You" was a big hit for The Flamingos in 1959, yet here Grace and James are dancing to it in 1955. One last point: in the opening credits, Meredith Salenger's last name is misspelled "Salinger."

MUSIC/BANDS: When Buffy turns down Ben's invitation to the Sadie Hawkins Dance at The Bronze, the music playing is "Charge," by the band Splendid. "I Only Have Eyes For You," performed by The Flamingos, plays when Buffy sees Grace and James dancing, and when she and Angel resolve the conflict the song is playing again. The song can be found on numerous oldies compilation albums. Score by Christophe Beck.

BEST POP CULTURE REFERENCE: When Buffy stops the first guy from shooting his girlfriend: "You just went O.J. on your girlfriend." There's really no explanation needed for that one.

2.20 Go Fish

ORIGINAL AIR DATE: May 5, 1998
WRITTEN BY: David Fury and Elin Hampton
DIRECTED BY: David Semel

GUEST CAST: Armin Shimerman as Principal Snyder
Charles Cyphers as Coach Marin

Jeremy Garrett as Cameron Walker
Wentworth Miller as Gage Petronzi
Conchata Ferrell as Nurse Greenleigh
Danny Strong as Jonathan
Shane West as Sean
Jake Patellis as Dodd McAlvy

Buffy and the gang must figure out what's going on when members of Sunnydale's champion swim team begin turning into sea creatures.

"Go Fish" was clearly a filler show before the season finale, so it lacked the clever ideas and symbolic parallels that most of the episodes contain. Nonetheless, it had its moments.

One of the biggest double standards in high school is the star treatment athletes get while the academics go largely ignored. Perhaps pep rallies are a way of giving football jocks something to cling to years down the road when they're pumping gas, but considering high school is when emotions are at their shakiest and lifelong impressions are made, the eggheads will never be treated as well as the athletes.

In "Go Fish" the writers explore the perks an athlete gets in high school, showing how those advantages have detrimental effects on others. Gage would rather play erotic solitaire than write computer programs, but Principal Snyder orders Willow to pass him. Knowing how difficult it is for Willow to lie about anything, and considering that she happens to be a brainy student who has always worked for her marks, he has given her a daunting task. Meanwhile, Buffy is almost sexually assaulted by Cameron, who is let off the hook because Snyder says her clothing was too provocative. The most disturbing thing about the incident is the lack of compassion the gang shows Buffy. As she stands and complains, they all give her that "won't-you-please-shut-up" look, as if being violated is an everyday occurrence. Sure, in that situation Buffy will always be far more dangerous than the perpetrator, but that doesn't negate the seriousness of the incident.

The best part about this episode were the giant steps Xander and Cordelia take in their relationship. In "Killed By Death" they moved beyond just kissing to actually caring for one another, but in this episode the speech Cordelia makes to "Xander" is astounding, to say the least. When faced with the possibility of Xander turning into a sea creature, Cordelia expresses her normal selfish concerns about how dating such a thing would affect her social status. Yet when she thinks the sea creature in the pool *is* Xander, she tells him that she'll still date him and help him adapt to his new lifestyle. Does she say

EVERETT COLLECTION/WARNER BROS.

it out of fear? No, because if she truly feared the creature she would have run, rather than follow him down the length of the pool pouring her heart out to him. Perhaps she has a newfound attraction to him after seeing him in the Speedos (easily the most memorable scene in the episode), but her conviction seems to go beyond that.

"Go Fish" is an entertaining episode, despite lacking depth, and offers viewers one last moment of levity before the series launches into its breathtaking season finale.

HIGHLIGHT: Willow's interrogation of Jonathan, showing her new sense of authority.

NITPICKS: Cordelia and Xander used the phrase "ran like a girl," when in fact the toughest person in their lives *is* a girl. "Ran like a wuss" would have been more appropriate. Also, when the coach pushes Buffy in with the sea creatures he says they've already eaten, insinuating they are full and need a sexual plaything. So when Buffy pushes the coach in and immediately comments on how the boys *really* love their coach, does she mean what we think she means? Finally, at the end, when the sea creatures are swimming out to the ocean, why are they such exceptionally bad swimmers?

OOPS: There are four sea creatures, yet as you watch them swim out to the ocean there are only three. Also, Cordelia says it's about time the school excelled at something, yet way back in "Teacher's Pet" Blaine tells Ms. French he took the championships, and in "Some Assembly Required" Daryl Epps was on the championship football team.

MUSIC/BANDS: During the swim team's victory party on the beach, the song playing is Naked's "Mann Chinese," from their self-titled album. As Buffy spies on Gage at The Bronze, the song is "If You'd Listen" by Nero's Rome, from their album, *Togetherly*. Score by Sean Murray and Shawn Clement.

BEST POP CULTURE REFERENCE: Cordelia says she doesn't want to date the creature from the blue lagoon, and Xander corrects her: "Black lagoon! The creature from the blue lagoon was Brooke Shields." Cordelia has mixed up the 1954 horror film *Creature from the Black Lagoon* with the 1980 horrific teen romance flick *The Blue Lagoon*, where Brooke Shields is trapped on a desert island with Christopher Atkins. It was an understandable error, actually.

ORIGINAL AIR DATE: May 12, 1998
WRITTEN BY: Joss Whedon
DIRECTED BY: Joss Whedon

GUEST CAST: Seth Green as Oz
Julie Benz as Darla
Bianca Lawson as Kendra
James Marsters as Spike
Juliet Landau as Drusilla
Armin Shimerman as Principal Snyder
Max Perlich as Whistler
Jack McGee as Doug Perren
Richard Riehle as LA Watcher
Shannon Welles as Gypsy Woman
Zitto Kazann as Gypsy Man

As Angel and Drusilla try to open the hellmouth to engulf the earth, the pasts of the show's key players flash before our eyes.

The basis of "Becoming," like "Passion," is in the title. We see how Angel became a vampire, how he got a soul, how Buffy became a slayer, and how Angel became her guardian. This absolutely brilliant episode gave viewers something they've been begging for — a look into the past to see what made these characters who they are. The only downside is we don't see how Giles became a watcher, but that's because it had no bearing on the overall plot line, which focused on the Buffy/Angel relationship. As wonderful as it is, though, any look into the past will emphasize a show's inconsistencies (see "OOPS" section).

Once again a voice-over narration is used to superb effect. This time it is Whistler, a great new character (who viewers hope will return in the third season) whose background and reason for being there seem to go largely unexplained, other than that he's some sort of good demon sent by somebody to help Angel (how's that for specifics?). Whistler is played by Max Perlich — a dead ringer for Thom Yorke of Radiohead — who is best known for his recurring role as Brodie on *Homicide: Life on the Street* and as a character actor in movies like *Maverick* and *Beautiful Girls*. Whistler is the third turning point in Angel's life, helping him become a useful member of society. Because he seems to know what is going on in the past and present, he is the perfect candidate for narrator.

Going back in time is a fascinating experience (although we must thank our lucky stars that Angel lost that dreadful phony accent) as we see the torments Angel has caused other people, as well as the suffering that has been inflicted upon him. Joss brilliantly connects the past and present in these flashbacks — we move from a helpless Drusilla begging to be pure, to the Drusilla of the present, who is evil and completely out of her mind; Angel being given his soul cuts to Willow and Buffy finding Jenny's restoration spell; Angel watching Buffy in 1996 dissolves to Angel watching her now.

The most inconsistent of the flashbacks is the one where Buffy becomes the slayer. Considering this moment is set less than a year before the series' time line begins, why is she *so* different? 1996 Buffy is flighty, vacuous, and acts more like Cordelia than the Buffy we know. Are we to believe that Buffy instantly matured when she became the slayer? And, as mentioned earlier, in "Welcome to the Hellmouth" Angel acts like he's never seen Buffy before, whereas we discover here that he's been watching her the whole time.

The biggest moral dilemma is raised when Xander voices his anger at the thought of Buffy and Willow restoring Angel's soul. Xander's reaction borders on viciousness, even causing Giles to lunge at him. Is Xander jealous? Is he playing Devil's Advocate? Or does he have a point? Yes, Buffy is in love with Angel and it's the demon inside Angel that killed Jenny, but what if they do restore him? Will he lose his soul again if he achieves *another* moment of happiness? Or can Willow deliver the spell in a way that prevents that from happening? Buffy loves Angel, who was a good person to have on the gang's side. On the other hand, the evil Angelus is a very dangerous monster. This is one moment on *Buffy* where there is no clear right or wrong, and the characters are completely divided. Giles wants to cast the spell to fulfill Jenny's last wish, Buffy wants to be reunited with her love, and Xander doesn't want the spell to be cast, partly because of his jealousy of Angel — all of them are clearly ruled by their passions here. Only Willow refuses to take a side.

The end of this episode is very powerful, especially when the scene goes into slow motion to stretch out Buffy's arrival at the disaster scene. (Does Joss know how to savor the moment or what?) The music is so effective at this moment, it almost becomes a character itself. Kendra is dead, Xander and Willow are unconscious, Cordelia is gone, and Giles has been kidnapped. Just as Whistler says, you can never be ready for moments like this one. Buffy has probably imagined such a moment many times, but she's never been prepared for it. This episode concludes with a real cliffhanger, one which Joss resolves beautifully in the finale.

HIGHLIGHT: The reappearance of Darla at the beginning.

NITPICKS: Giles uses something as important as an Orb of Thessala for a paperweight? As potentially funny as that is, it seems strange he wouldn't have offered it earlier for the restoration spell. Also, why didn't we see how Spike became a vampire, or are they saving that until later? And finally, Kendra calls her stake Mr. Pointy? That dialogue was pretty lame, and out of character for Kendra.

OOPS: Angel is 242 years old, which would place his birth date in 1756. Yet in this episode he is turned into a vampire in 1753 — someone's math is way off. The time line with other episodes is thrown off as well. In "Nightmares," Buffy tells Willow that her parents divorced the previous year (which would have been 1996) but were separated for a while before that. Yet in this episode her parents are fighting and still living together in 1996. And in "Angel," Angel tells Buffy he was a demon for 100 years, when in fact it was closer to 150.

INTERESTING FACT: "Becoming" won the 1998 Technical Emmy for Music Competition for a Series (Dramatic Underscore).

MUSIC/BANDS: Score by Christophe Beck.

2.22 Becoming 2

ORIGINAL AIR DATE: May 19, 1998
WRITTEN BY: Joss Whedon
DIRECTED BY: Joss Whedon

GUEST CAST: Seth Green as Oz
Kristine Sutherland as Joyce Summers
Robia LaMorte as Ms. Calendar
James Marsters as Spike
Juliet Landau as Drusilla
Armin Shimerman as Principal Snyder
Max Perlich as Whistler
James G. MacDonald as Detective Stein
Susan Leslie as First Cop
Thomas G. Waites as Second Cop

As Angel tortures Giles and Willow re-attempts the restoration spell, Buffy prepares to kill Angel.

What can I say? The master of television has outdone himself again. Joss, you are a god. This season finale leaves the viewer breathless, depleted, and begging for answers.

Both Buffy and Giles show how strong-willed they are; the more that is taken from them, the more difficult it is to break them. As pointed out earlier, Giles survives the physical torture because Jenny has already been taken from him, which is the worst torture he's ever endured. Buffy becomes a fugitive, gets kicked out of the home, has friends in the hospital, and is expelled from school, but steels herself against it all to fulfill her duty. However, as Whistler tells her, she's got one more thing to lose, and even she couldn't have anticipated what that would be.

The biggest turning point in the show is that Joyce discovers Buffy is the slayer. Next season will be very different now that Joyce is in on the big secret — the show's dynamic is forever changed. Buffy's secret represents all those things that teenagers keep from their parents, and now that secret is revealed, it will be interesting to see where Buffy and Joyce go from here. It is difficult to imagine what it must have been like for Joyce to hear Buffy's news, and what's worse, Buffy doesn't take the time to explain herself. She's in the house and on the phone, leaving Joyce to sit in the living room with Spike and try to decide whether her daughter is completely delusional. Your first instinct may be to chastise Joyce for her treatment of Buffy or wonder why she didn't figure it out sooner, but ask yourself this: What would *you* do if your son or daughter told you that vampires were real and he or she had been chosen to defend the world from them?

Spike is wonderful here. From his attempt to reason with Buffy (while trying to fend off her blows), to his explanation that Buffy plays the triangle in his rock band, to his assault on Dru, he becomes a multifaceted character ripe for development next season (Spike and Dru will return). While Spike was largely ignored in "Becoming," he returns with a vengeance in this one.

And what of the end of the episode? Do we blame Xander for not telling Buffy the truth? Either he was jealous of Angel or he knew that Buffy wouldn't fight as hard if she thought Angel's soul would be restored. Notice how Buffy held back during their last fight, waiting for the spell to kick in. Do we blame Willow for trying the spell in the first place? If Willow hadn't restored Angel's soul, Buffy would have annihilated him and closed the hellmouth without having her heart ripped out. How about Giles? He is the one, after all, who told Angel the secret to awake Acathla, without which Buffy wouldn't have had to kill Angel. But can we blame someone who was so overwhelmed by love he momentarily lost his senses? The truth is, everyone was looking out for Buffy, but their actions ended up causing Buffy the worst pain imaginable.

Sarah Michelle Gellar delivered her best performance yet, as did Anthony Stewart Head. This season has been a roller-coaster for all the characters, and the writing, directing, and music were amazing. Cordy and Xander kiss for the first time in a meaningful and caring way, and Willow calls out to Oz rather than Xander. If Season Three delivers half of what we got in "Becoming 2," we're in for a treat.

All television shows should be this good.

HIGHLIGHT: The uncomfortable silence between Joyce and Spike in the living room, and Xander's speech to an unconscious Willow.

NITPICKS: How did Buffy know that Drusilla killed Kendra? And at the end, Spike appeared to be driving like he was in a bumper car, not on the road.

OOPS: One of the many things that makes this show stand above all other action shows is how similar the body and stunt doubles are to the actors. Unfortunately, when Angel is swordfighting with Buffy, you can tell exactly when it's the double and when it's Boreanaz: just look at the sideburns on the double. Also, notice how Buffy's hairstyle keeps changing during the fight scene.

MUSIC/BANDS: As Buffy leaves Sunnydale, the beautiful song in the background is Sarah McLachlan's "Full of Grace," from her CD *Surfacing*. Score by Christophe Beck.

BEST POP CULTURE REFERENCE: Spike tells Buffy that the world is a good place because of all its people, saying, "Millions of people walking around like Happy Meals with legs," a reference to the children's meals at McDonald's.

"Grr . . . Argh."

TRIVIA ANSWERS

RANK

95–100	The Chosen One
85–94	Watcher
70–84	Slayerette
50–69	Vampire
20–49	Vampire Wannabe
0–19	Joyce Summers

XANDERISMS

Score one point for each correct answer.

1. "Killed By Death"
2. "I Only Have Eyes For You"
3. "Bewitched, Bothered and Bewildered"
4. "The Witch"
5. "Innocence"
6. "When She Was Bad"
7. "Some Assembly Required"
8. "Surprise"
9. "School Hard"
10. "I Only Have Eyes For You"

WHAT'S MY LINE?

Score half a point for correctly answering who said the line and half a point for getting the episode right.

1. Giles in "Teacher's Pet" (to an inmate of an insane asylum)
2. Buffy in "Bewitched, Bothered and Bewildered" (to Oz)
3. Cordelia in "What's My Line?" (to Xander)
4. Spike in "Lie to Me" (to Ford)
5. Buffy in "The Harvest" (upon realizing the vampires were coming out of the mausoleum)
6. Giles in "Never Kill a Boy on the First Date" (to Buffy)
7. Principal Flutie in "Teacher's Pet" (to Buffy)
8. Willow in "Lie to Me" (to Angel)
9. Oz in "Innocence" (to Willow)

10. Angel in "Passion" (to Spike)
11. Buffy in "What's My Line?" (to Kendra)
12. Principal Snyder in "The Puppet Show" (to the gang)
13. Spike in "School Hard" (to Angel)
14. Buffy in "The Pack" (to Willow and Giles)
15. Cordelia in "Bewitched, Bothered and Bewildered" (to Xander)
16. Ted in "Ted" (to Buffy)
17. Buffy in "Becoming 2" (to Whistler)
18. Cordelia in "Invisible Girl" (to the gang)
19. Angel in "Angel" (to Darla)
20. Willow in "Go Fish" (to the gang)

WHO'S WHO?

Score one point for each correct answer.

1. He was in the stacks when Giles and Buffy were talking about her duties.
2. He was killed by vampires, along with four others, while traveling in a bus, fulfilling a prophecy that out of the death of five would arise the One.
3. Ira Rosenberg. We find this out in "Passion."
4. Prague.
5. Barely 200 years old, according to Giles.
6. Morgan ("The Puppet Show") and Ford ("Lie to Me").
7. Giles, who mentions it in "The Dark Age."
8. To play a D°9 (D diminished 9th) chord.
9. Ted.
10. Jonathan.
11. A good demon who has been sent to guide Angel.
12. She got trapped inside the cheerleading trophy.
13. Cordelia.
14. Darla.
15. She had just taken her final vows at a convent.

EPISODE EVENTS

Score one point for each correct answer, unless otherwise indicated.

1. "Inca Mummy Girl" and "Bewitched, Bothered and Bewildered" (2 points)
2. Delta Beta Kappa
3. Listens to country music — "The music of pain"
4. The cockroach fumigation party

5. "Was it good for you?"
6. "The Witch" and "Phases" (2 points)
7. "Ted" and "Becoming 2" (2 points)
8. A woman who is smoking in the alleyway
9. "Phases"
10. How to properly eat a Twinkie
11. "Bewitched, Bothered and Bewildered" and "What's My Line? Part Two" (2 points)
12. A large sword
13. "The Harvest"
14. "Lie to Me"
15. "What's My Line? Part Two" and "Phases" (2 points)
16. "Teacher's Pet"
17. "Prophecy Girl" and "Passion" (2 points)
18. Taking the icing out of an Oreo cookie, "without the chocolatey cookie goodness"
19. "I Only Have Eyes For You"
20. "Reptile Boy" and "What's My Line? Part Two" (2 points)
21. "Inca Mummy Girl" and "Halloween" (2 points)
22. Fighting another vampire

THERE'S A FIRST TIME FOR EVERYTHING

Score one point for each correct answer.

1. "Phases" (moonpie joke)
2. "Angel" (on the dance floor)
3. "Some Assembly Required" (to the football game)
4. "Prophecy Girl" when she saves Ms. Calendar and Willow from the vampires
5. "Angel"
6. "Nightmares"
7. "Never Kill a Boy on the First Date" (Owen)
8. "Surprise" (at Buffy's party)
9. "Bad Eggs"
10. "Invisible Girl"
11. "Bewitched, Bothered and Bewildered"
12. "The Harvest"
13. "The Witch"
14. "Halloween" (they bump into each other in the hallway while Willow is dressed as a ghost and apologize to each other). Give yourself half a point if you said "What's My Line?" where they first speak to each other and actually know it.
15. "Angel" (at the hospital after Joyce is bitten)

TRUE OR FALSE?

1. False. He dropped out before he could finish the program.
2. False. Willow says that. Buffy doesn't even know who Dickinson is.
3. True.
4. False. Buffy never tells him about the tattoo and removes it at her own expense.
5. False. She used to play the piano.
6. False. He pretended not to remember because he didn't want to admit to what he'd done to Buffy and Willow. Xander wasn't with the pack when Principal Flutie was eaten.
7. True.
8. False. Cordelia doesn't have a sister, to our knowledge.
9. False. At her last school, she was voted May Queen.
10. False. His cousin is a werewolf.

SOURCES

Anderson, Dennis. "Vampire-Slayer Buffy Battles Master." *The Associated Press*. May 29, 1997.

"Anthony Head." *The Transylvanian Conventions — 1992 Guests*. Online. July 3, 1998.

Barber, Paul. *Vampires, Burial, and Death: Folklore and Reality*. New Haven: Yale UP, 1988.

Boreanaz, David. Interview with Keenan Ivory Wayans. *The Keenan Ivory Wayans Show*. Fox. California.

____. Interview with Regis Philbin and Kathie Lee Gifford. *Live With Regis and Kathie Lee*. ABC.

Boris, Cynthia. "Anthony Stewart Head is Watching Buffy." *Mania*. Online. May 3, 1998.

____. "*Buffy the Vampire Slayer*'s Robia La Morte and Robin Sachs: A Re-Occurrence in Sunnydale." *Mania*. Online. May 3, 1998.

Brady, James. "Sarah Michelle Gellar." *Parade Magazine*. July 6, 1997.

"Breakthroughs '97 — Sarah Michelle Gellar." *People*. December 29, 1997.

Brendon, Nicholas. Interview with Sinbad. *Vibe*. CBS. May 4, 1998.

"*Buffy the Vampire Slayer*'s David Boreanaz." BBS Bulletin Board Chat. September 17, 1997. TV *Guide*. Online. June 15, 1998.

" 'Buffy' Tunes Into Teens." *New York Daily News*. March 30, 1997.

Carpenter, Charisma. Interview with Keenan Ivory Wayans. *The Keenan Ivory Wayans Show*. Fox. California. January 8, 1998.

Carson, Tom. "Buffy Battles Teendom's Demons." *The Village Voice*. June 7, 1997.

Carter, Alan. "Young Love in the Afternoon." *Entertainment Weekly*. 1992.

"Charisma Carpenter Star Chat." *UltimateTV*. April 15, 1997. Online. May 15, 1998.

"The Claddagh Ring." *Claddagh Jewellers*. Online. July 3, 1998.

Cobo, Father Bernake. *Inca Religion and Customs*. Trans. and Ed. Roland Hamilton. Austin: U of Texas P, 1990.

Collymore, Terrie. "Teen Queen." *Soap Opera Digest*. 1994.

Day, John. *Molech: A God of Human Sacrifice in the Old Testament*. Cambridge: Cambridge UP, 1989.

Decker, Sean. "Interview with the Vampire Slayer." October 1997. *Dungeon of Darkness*. Online. March 31, 1998.

Decker, Sean J. "An Interview with Kevin Williamson." October 5, 1997. *Horror Movie*. Online. June 13, 1998.

"Do As the Roma Do." *Soap Opera Weekly*. 1993.

Douglas, Adam. *The Beast Within*. London: Chapmans, 1992.

Douglas, Drake. *Horrors!* Woodstock, NY: Overlook, 1989.

Dunn, Jancee. "Love at First Bite: Sarah Michelle Gellar." *Rolling Stone*. April 2, 1998.

Ferrante, Anthony C. "New Kicks for Buffy the Vampire Slayer." *Fangoria*. January 1998.

Fienberg, Daniel. "*Buffy* Goes Prime Time." *The Daily Pennsylvanian*. April 10, 1997.

"Friends." *Soap Opera Weekly*. 1993.

Gellar, Sarah Michelle. Interviewed by David Letterman. *Late Show with David Letterman*. CBS. New York. November 20, 1997.

____. Interviewed by Howard Stern. *The Howard Stern Show*. March 10, 1998.

____. Interviewed by Jay Leno. *The Tonight Show with Jay Leno*. NBC. New York. September 8, 1997.

____. Interviewed by Jay Leno. *The Tonight Show with Jay Leno*. NBC. New York. December 17, 1997.

____. Interviewed by Rosie O'Donnell. *The Rosie O'Donnell Show*. ABC. February 17, 1998.

Good News Bible. Toronto: Canadian Bible Society, 1976.

Goods, Lorraine. "Sarah Michelle Gellar: Cult of the Vampire." *People*. Online. March 18, 1998.

Gordon, Stuart. *The Encyclopedia of Myths and Legends*. London: Headline, 1994.

Graham, Jefferson. "*Buffy* Star Likes Demands of Action-Comedy Role." *USA Today*. March 28, 1997.

____. "The Ratings Slayer: Box Office Bomb Has Turned Into a Hit on Television." *USA Today*. March 28, 1997.

Graham, Jennifer and Jeanne Wolf. "Slay Anything." *YM*. January 1998.

Green, Michelle. "Stake-ing a Claim in *The Vampire Slayer*." *Mania*. Online. May 3, 1998.

Green, Michelle Erica. "Werewolf of Sunnydale: The Wizard of Oz." *Mania*. Online. May 3, 1998.

Grimal, Pierre. *The Dictionary of Classical Mythology*. Trans. A.R. Maxwell. Oxford: Blackwell, 1996.

Hensley, Dennis. "Miracle Worker." *Movieline*. November 1997.

Hine, Thomas. "TV's teen-agers: They're insecure, world-weary and (of course) misunderstood." November 10, 1997. *Houston Chronicle*. Online. March 31, 1998.

Hobson, Louis B. "To Die For." *Calgary Sun*. December 1, 1997.

The Internet Movie Database. Online.

"Interview with the Cast of *Swans Crossing*." *Teen Party*. 1992.

Kemp, Anthony. *Witchcraft and Paganism Today*. London: Michael O'Mara, 1993.

Krantz, Michael. "The Bard of Gen-Y." December 15, 1997. *Time*. Online. June 13, 1998.

Kutzera, Dale. "Sarah Michelle Gellar is the Heroine Who Battles Monsters and Teen Angst." *Femme Fatales*. July 1997.

"Like Mother, Like Daughter." *Daytime TV*. 1994.

Littleton, Cynthia. "FX Network Bags *Buffy* Reruns at $650,000 Per Episode." *Variety*. February 25, 1998.

"Live Star Chat with Seth Green." *UltimateTV*. Online. June 15, 1998.

Lyons, Shelly. "Alyson Hannigan's 'Willow' — Wallflower by Day, Assistant Slayer by Night." *UltimateTV*. Online. May 11, 1998.

Malkin, Marc S. "Lucky Dog!" *Twist*. April/May 1998.

Martinez, Jose. "Buffy's Screaming Good Summer Vacation." *Venice*. October 1997.

Maslin, Janet. "Steamy TV: Coffee Opera." *The New York Times*. November 22, 1992.

Miller, Bruce R. "Staking a Claim." *Sioux City Journal*. March 7, 1997.

Milton, John. *Paradise Lost*. 1674. Merritt Y. Hughes, ed. New York: Macmillan, 1989.

Moore, Frazier. "High School Horrific." TV *Week — The Washington Post*. March 30, 1997.

Moseley, Michael E. *The Incas and Their Ancestors: The Archaeology of Peru*. London: Thames and Hudson, 1992.

Noll, Richard. *Vampires, Werewolves, and Demons: Twentieth Century Reports in the Psychiatric Literature*. New York: Brunner/Mazel, 1992.

Norton, Peter B. et al, eds. *The New Encyclopedia Britannica*. 15th ed. Chicago: Encyclopedia Britannica, Inc., 1995. 29 vols.

Owen, Rob. "High School Horror on *Buffy the Vampire Slayer*: Teen Angst Trumps the Supernatural." *Albany Time Union*. September 15, 1997.

"Passion — Alyson Hannigan: Beanie Babies." *Teen People*. April 1998.

Pearlman, Cindy. "Interview with Sarah Michelle Gellar." *Chicago Sun-Times*. September 1997.

Persons, Mitch. "*Buffy the Vampire Slayer*, Bringing classic horror to a whole new audience." *Cinefantastique*. March 1998.

"Petcabus Awards." *The Petcabus Awards Homepage*. Online. July 6, 1998.

Pierce, Scott D. "Buffy is Way Cool." *Deseret News*. June 2, 1997.

____. "Role on *Buffy* has opened delightful new world for actor." *Deseret News*. June 5, 1998.

Queenan, Joe. "High Stakes." TV *Guide*. May 17-23, 1997.

Rochlin, Margy and Lawless. "Slay Belle." TV *Guide*. August 2-8, 1997.

Roesch, Scott. "Sarah's Summer." *Mr. Showbiz*. Online. March 18, 1998.

Rudolph, Amanda. "He's a Keeper." *InStyle*. May 1998.

Rudwin, Maximilian. *The Devil in Legend and Literature*. 1931. La Salle, Illinois: Open Court, 1989.

Rush, Michael S. "Learning Life's Lessons." *Daytime* TV. 1993.

Schorow. Stephanie. "Stakeout." *The Boston Herald*. May 19, 1997.

Sebald, Hans. *Witch-Children: From Salem Witch-Hunts to Modern Courtrooms*. Amherst: Prometheus, 1995.

Senn, Harry. *The Were-Wolf and Vampire in Romania*. Boulder: East European Monographs, 1982.

Sloane, Judy. "Alyson Hannigan." *Xposé*. December 1997.

Solin, Sabrina. "Girl Meets Boy." *Seventeen Magazine*. August 1994.

"Star Boards — Sarah Michelle Gellar." *E!* Online. March 31, 1998.

Steinbach, Sheila. "Daytime's Hottest Young Stars." *Soap Opera Update*. 1993.

Strauss, Bob. "*Buffy* Star Sarah Gellar Nurtures Her Film Career." *Detroit Free Press*. November 10, 1997.

Thomas, Mike. "A Virtual Gentleman: Anthony Head says goodbye to his 'nice guy' image in VR.5." *Cult Times*. 2

Thompson, Bob. "She Buffs Up the Teenage Image." *Toronto Sun*. December 3, 1997.

196

Thompson, Malissa. "Interview with Sarah Michelle Gellar." *React*. October 27-November 2, 1997.

Tong, Diane. *Gypsy Folktales*. San Diego: Harcourt, 1989.

Turner, Alice K. *The History of Hell*. New York: Harcourt, 1993.

Wolf, Jeanne. "Listen Up with Sarah Michelle Gellar." *TV Guide*. Online. March 31, 1998.

____. "Q&A with Charisma Carpenter." *TV Guide*. Online. May 7, 1998.

____. "Q&A with Sarah Michelle Gellar." *TV Guide*. Online. March 31, 1998.

____. "Q&A with Nicholas Brendon." *TV Guide*. Online. June 15, 1998.

Yovanovich, Linda. "Young Blood." *OnSat*. July 14, 1997.